Harbinger
Book One of Northern Fire

Harbinger
Book One of Northern Fire

Ian H. McKinley

Harbinger: Book One of Northern Fire
© Ian H. McKinley, 2016
© This edition Lugar Común Editorial, 2020
Gerardo Barajas-Garrido, Collection Editor for Ojo de Vidrio

*Publishers note: This book is a work of fiction. All names, characters,
places and incidents either are the product of the author's imagination
or are used fictitiously, and any resemblance to actual persons living
or dead, events, or locales is entirely coincidental.*

Library and Archives Canada Cataloguing in Publication

ISBN 978-1-987819-47-2

First Published in 2016
2nd Edition Lugar Común Editorial, Collection Ojo de Vidrio

Ottawa, Canada, 2020

www.lugarcomuneditorial.com
info@lugarcomuneditorial.com

Canada

for William McKinley, my brother,
who taught me that heart conquers skill,
and in memory of my father, William Harold McKinley,
who taught me to enjoy life
and who re-discovered that joy before the end.

Table of contents

Dramatis Personae

The principal characters:
Harbinger recounts the coming of age of four children, though they do not dominate the narrative until Part II: The Tithe of the Sea Wolves.
-Lars Sorenith, son of Renith and Rena;
-Cairn Soleigh, son of Leigh and Fallig;
-Lora Dauilig, daughter of Uilig and Loska; and,
-Thay Sorig, son of Rig and Thülla.

The Darnok of Krannogberg:
Prominent people who populate the town of Krannogberg:
-Hondsar Sogale, the ill-fated chieftain of the Darnok;
-Knab Sokilg, the man who succeeds Hondsar as the Darnok's chieftain;
-Helgya Darik, the Darnok's legendary seeress and healer;
-Loska Daeinar, Deputy to Knab in the defence of Krannogberg and mother to Lora;
-Magon Sokirth, Priest of Hondrig, Krannogberg's spiritual guide; and,
-Kyre Sobelden, Krannogberg's bard.

The Arctic Wolves clan of the Sea Wolves:
-Kindron Sopallig, chieftain of the Arctic Wolves and captain of the longship *Rignil*;
-Asgear Solief, Kindron's first officer on *Rignil*;
-Krüllig Sohygar, crewman on *Rignil*;
-Toftig Soaghen, captain of the longship *Thunderer*;
-Albig Soragnar, captain of the longship *Northern Fire*;
-Niers Sodjernen, the Arctic Wolves' Priest of Hondrig;
-Erig Soerig, the Arctic Wolves' bard; and,
-Bjarni Sohenkel, a scarred Sea Wolf.

Some other personages in this work:
-Rigald Sokaroth, Chieftain of the Jarlags, a rival clan to the Darnok who live in Sangspit, on Caljürd's Arm, south of Krannogberg;
-Yens Hezteins, a Straelish slave on board Rignil, formerly a *herg* (lord) in his home country;
-*Oberherg* Skindler, a Straelish *oberherg* (duke).

A Note on Fjordlander Last Names

At the point of time depicted in this work, Fjordland was still all too patriarchal and the last name a Fjordlander bore related back to the first name of his or her father.

If the child was female, then her last name was constructed first with a prefix "Da" a more-quickly stated contraction of "Daughter of." Then came her father's given name. The name of the clan did not normally feature in this construction. In this work, one Fjordlander female is prominent:

Lora Dauilig (Lora, daughter of Uilig)

If the child was male, then his last name featured the same construction based on his father's name, except that the prefix was "So" for "Son of." Again, three Fjordlander males are prominent:

Cairn Soleigh (Cairn, son of Leigh);
Lars Sorenith (Lars, son of Renith); and,
Thay Sorig (Thay, son of Rig).

Notes on Fjordlander Theology

For those readers who may wish to refer to them, at the end of this book appear some notes on the pantheon of Fjordlander gods.

Map of the Northlands

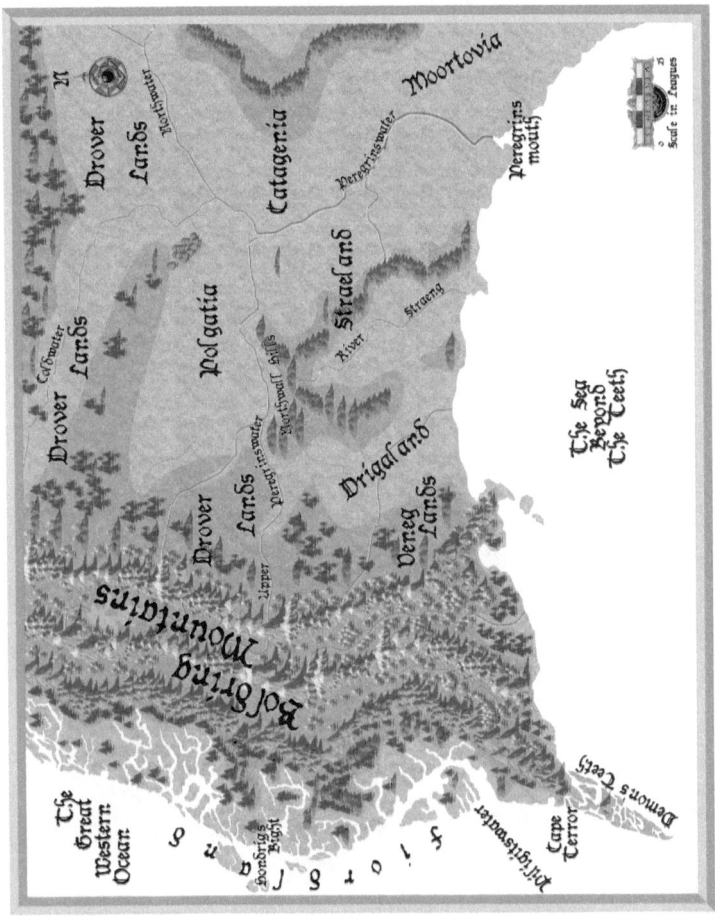

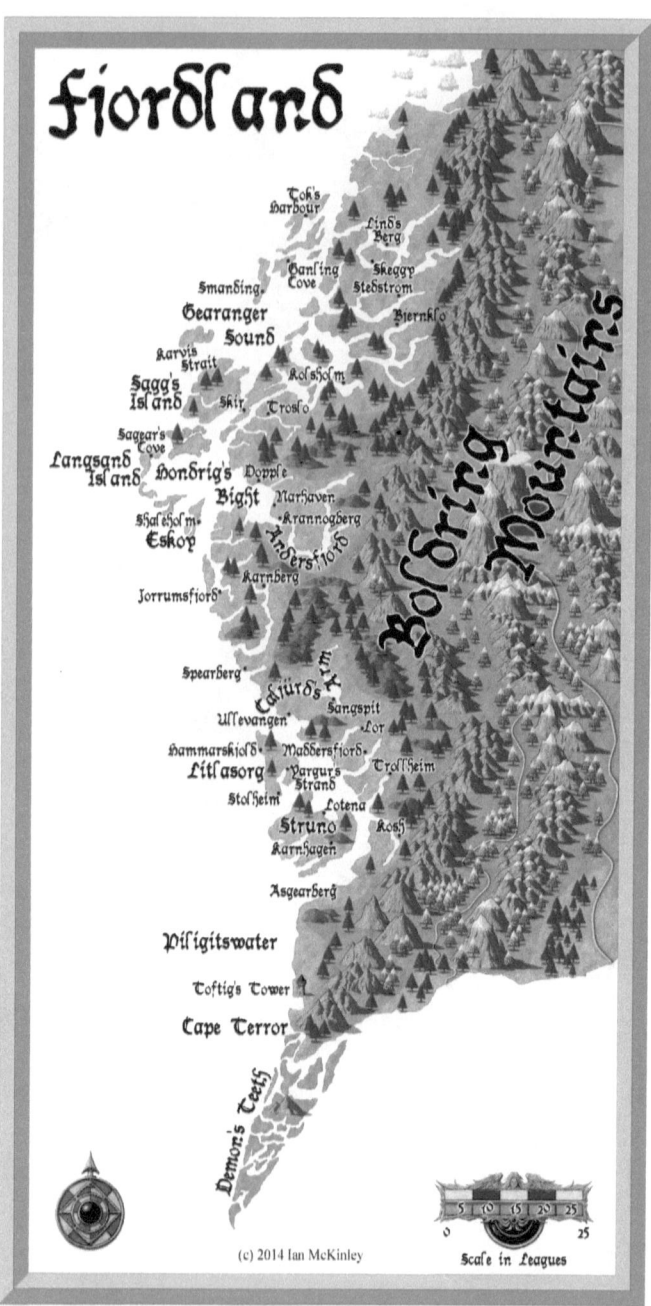

fiordland

Tok's Harbour
Lind's Berg
Smanding
Hanling Cove
Skeggy Stedstrom
Gearanger Sound
Biernklo
Karvis Strait
Kolsholm
Sagg's Island
Skir
Troslo
Sagear's Cove
Langsand Island
Hondrig's Bight
Dopple
Marhaven
Krannogberg
Skafsholm
Eskoy
Andersfiord
Karnberg
Jorrumsfiord
Spearberg
Thjürd's Arm
Sangspit
Ullevangen
Lor
Hammarskjold's
Maddersfiord
Trollheim
Litlasorg
Vargur's Strand
Stolheim
Lotena
Struno
Ross
Karnhagen
Asgearberg
Pilfigitswater
Toftig's Tower
Cape Terror
Demon's Teeth
Bosdring Mountains

(c) 2014 Ian McKinley

5 10 15 20 25
0   25
Scale in Leagues

Map of Hondrig's Bight & Surrounds

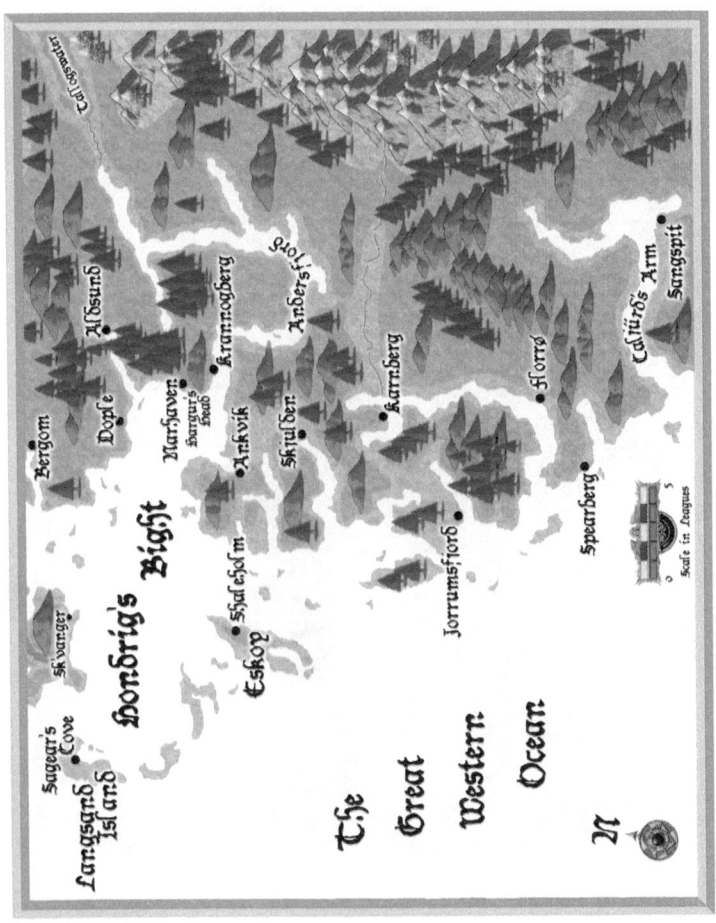

Map of Fjorland (left)

Map of the Kingdom of Straeland

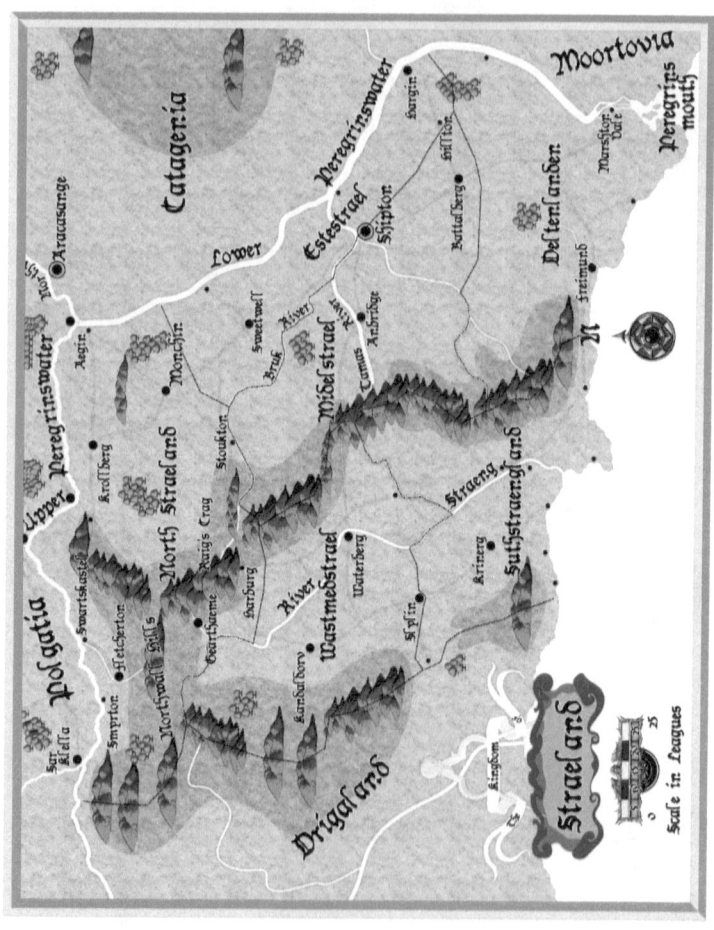

Prologue

A great deal of wailing occurred that fateful Darknight, the night of midwinter, though for once the folk of Krannogberg could blame neither the Jarlags nor the Sea Wolves. No one came raiding with fiery brands and no one rowed off into Hondrig's Bight carrying away a bitter tithe. No creature brought death to the Darnok on behalf of Sk'van, the demon who revels in misery. No ice storm rolled over the Andersfjord shedding Tears of the Ghosts - for neither god nor devil would shed anything so cold - collapsing roofs and making pathways treacherous. That night only snow fell from the Godspace. No, the wailing was due to more mundane, and hopeful, reasons. A remarkable thing happened that long, frigid night; four women gave birth. Common birthings occurred from time to time, usually nine months after Gods' Day celebrations or festivals tied to the position of the sun. But never before in all the collective stories of the clan had four women come to term the very same night, let alone on Darknight.

While the settlement celebrated half a winter put behind them, Helgya Darik, the village's seeress and midwife, ran from one cottage to another, tending to each woman as best she could. The Darnok would have feasted anyway; celebrations kept Sk'van away from birthings, a time when women walked close to Skalaag, the Domain of the Dead. The women clearly needed the protection of hollered toasts and raucous cheers, for all four birthings were hard-fought battles. Torga Danail, another respected woman helping Helgya, heard the seeress mutter, "The *wyrds* of the Gods Themselves must be in those four bairns for all the sweat and blood it's taking to bring them into the world."

Helgya, Torga, and the other women who helped, managed to keep their charges hale, or perhaps the town's revelry truly frightened off Sk'van or any other demon, for the women's wails ended just before dawn. Other wailing, though, echoed off the walls of the fjord; that of four lusty children.

Before she retired to her bed, Helgya fell to the floor of one of the cottages. Torga and others went to help the exhausted woman but Magon Sokirth, the village's Priest of Hondrig, cried out, "Hold! Approach not where Gods abide!" The women backed off, for priests and priestesses are sacred, manipulate the magic powers of the Gods, and are not to be gainsaid. Only Magon, with his full, grey beard that poured onto his broad chest, moved to Helgya. Some heard snippets of whispered words that passed Helgya's lips, but only Magon heard them clearly. If he had understood what she had gasped, he did not say. After he had carried Helgya to her cottage, Magon performed the welcoming rituals for the village's newest members: Lars, Cairn, Lora, and Thay.

When he finished, he walked through the village, his eyes hardly taking in the cottages made of wooden planks and with sloping roofs of either turf or shingles. His eyes did light on the wooden beams at the edge of the roofs, rising and crossing each other, and ending in sculpted likenesses of bears or wolves or dragons. Those likenesses were also meant to scare away demons and protect those who named the cottage home. As he passed revellers making their way across the muddy ground to those homes, dressed in their tunics and leggings, or in their long, thick dresses, he wondered if the beast heads could keep fate at bay. Magon walked out from the town, past the paddocks walled off by stacked stones, off across the newly fallen snow. He climbed half way up the fjord wall, to the Harrowood, and he sat in that grove of trees for the rest of the short day. Renith, Leigh, Uilig, and Rig also walked from the village that morning to give thought to their fortune. They slapped each other's backs, swigging draughts of ale from a cask they carried with them. They talked about what glorious future that Rulla, the Dealer of Fates, had bestowed on Krannogberg. None of them considered what that fate would cost them. But even had they known, three of them at least would all have agreed to the bargain, for men oft trade misery and hardship for names that live for generations.

The mothers - Rena, Fallig, Loska, and Thülla - finally lying asleep in their beds after their ordeals, might have tried to strike a different bargain with Rulla, Mistress of Owls, for She is known as a hard bargainer who stains each rune of glory She hands out in blood. And the runes She picked for the four young babies were not stained with blood, they were soaked in it.

Part I

A Sorrow Claw

Chapter One

The winter clung fiercely to the fjords that year, its claws sharper than those of the ice bear. Instead of rain and mud, snowdrifts and ice encased the slopes during the season following the remarkable Darknight of the four birthings. Winter passed more grudgingly than usual. Weeks past the time when the settlement's work normally started in earnest, fisher folk still only kept to the fjord, for icy winds blasted Hondrig's Bight and churned it into a cauldron that roiled with towering black waves. With snow still piled high on the plateau, cutting off the summer ranges on the slopes of the Boldring Mountains, the herders kept their sheep and cattle in their barns and hoped their hay would hold out.

During this time of work done around the burning hearth, the mothers of the four new babies often took care of their children together. Rena, Fallig, Loska, and Thülla were already friends and this time for them was one of increased bonding. Only Thülla had given birth before, to a girl, Ellena, and she imparted what wisdom she had gathered to the others. Fallig had undergone the most difficult birthing, for Cairn was a bulky babe, and the other three women lent her their strength until she had recuperated her own. For her, in particular, the long winter was a Gods-send; she would have had great difficulty making the trek to the mountains behind her herds. The women wondered at their good fortune in this and on their simultaneous birthings. They also speculated on what Helgya might have whispered in her trance; Magon had kept his silence and would not drop the slightest hint.

As soon as the snow disappeared from the plateau above the fjords, the herders took their charges up into the summer ranges. Leigh and Fallig left the settlement with Cairn wrapped up in a sheepskin and tucked safely beside his mother on the bench of their little two-wheeled horse cart. They drove their sheep straight for the valley that led to the High Pass. The going was slow, for more snow than usual during the winter had given way to more muck than usual on the track they followed, but they finally reached their summer cottage and found it in better shape than in any previous spring. Leigh had the place repaired and Fallig had it thoroughly cleaned within two days of their arrival. They took the condition of the cottage as a further sign that the winter had been a lucky one. When the snows had retreated from the High Pass, they took their child up to its summit, to the huge cairn of man height for which they had named their son. They presented the already substantial child to the stones there and offered thanks to Rulla for the fate She had bestowed upon them.

The other three babies remained in Krannogberg, for their fathers were fishers and took to the waves in search of a rich harvest of fish each day. Leigh and Fallig's good fortune must have spread to the village because the three men caught more fish than ever before on Hondrig's Bight. The parents of the three children also gave thanks to Rulla and prayed to Her if they saw one of Her fishing owls, for the bairns slept well, did not take ill and fed without trouble. Even the dour Magon came to believe that Florri, the God of Good Fortune, took special care of Krannogberg that year because no boats came back from the Bight rowing hard and yelling warnings, and no watchfires sprang to life from the Boldring Mountains.

Once Leigh and Fallig returned that autumn with a fat little Cairn in tow, the four mothers set to work on Magon. They badgered him whenever they could about Helgya's vision. They invited him to dinner with them while their husbands worked hewing and gathering wood for the winter. Despite the tradition that a priest would always enter a welcoming home, their prying reached such an intensity that Magon eventually declined their invitations. The women recruited their husbands to the cause and the men harassed the priest in his own home.

Finally, towards the arrival of Darknight, the winter solstice, Magon summoned the parents to the roundhouse. All four couples reacted with surprise when they arrived, for also present were the village council and Helgya. They grew grim and wondered at whatever Magon had to say to them. The grizzled old chieftain, Hondsar Sogale, beckoned them to sit around the central hearth and said, "All right Magon, my friend, tell me why you've summoned us here. I take it this has something to do with the four children born to us on one night last winter."

Magon nodded and replied, "Indeed. I have asked you all here because these eight parents have pressed me hard on the words Helgya spoke the morning following the birthings. I believe that the entire council should hear these words and consider them." The parents all cast quick glances at their spouses while Hondsar nodded. Magon turned his head to Helgya before continuing, "You have scried for us in the past but never from a trance. Is that not so?"

Helgya declared, "Aye. My verse comes to me unbidden and at times with visions that provide a clue to unlocking the words. Ach! I have no notion of what I spoke that day or any memory of any image that would help us suss this out."

"So you see," Magon stated, "we cannot turn to anything to help us understand Helgya's words. I say this because I cannot offer much in the way of interpretation myself. That morning, Helgya whispered the following words ..." Magon cleared his throat and pulled his sturdy frame erect before chanting:

Such sights I see as make me quake,
such woe for us as makes me weep:
a foreign lord with foreign arms
and sowing, here, foreign woes.

Such sights I see as make me fear,
such strife that rips us from our kin:
a choppy sea assailing reefs
and wrecking, there, Fjordland's folk.

Such sights I see as make me warn,
such swans of death that gorge on flesh:
a sorry clan on Jarlag ships
lest Darnok, quickly, gather here.

Such sights I see that make me hope,
such deeds so great they dull the grief:
a sorrow claw of rusting steel,
forsaken, here, on Darnok heath.

That sight is key to make me smile,
such light to chase the dark away:
three wielders fall from faithless steel,
to crown one here, a king's acclaim.

"I know not what to think of it," Magon continued. "It speaks not to me. The spirits offer no counsel. Now, it will be meaningless to you as well." Silence fell on the roundhouse. No one ventured any interpretation.

When finally the silence weighed too much, Rig, the father of Thay, said, "I do not see this future, should it prove true, as necessarily evil for us. She chanted the words 'lest Darnok quickly gather here.' It seems more a warning than anything else. No one has ever doubted that these bairns of ours have an important *wyrd* in front of them. We must do nothing foolish with them and just give them time to grow up, so they can make their own decisions, until the runes Rulla bestowed on them become clear to us." Heads nodded in agreement.

The parents all left the roundhouse in a sober mood. They did not dwell on their victory - that they had prodded Magon into sharing the words. Even so, it was an important victory, for without it Rig would never have thought to act upon those words. Twice.

§

When the time came to celebrate the babies' first birthing day, all of the settlement believed firmly that the four little ones had brought Florri's blessing, for not a single inhabitant had died that year and the village had been able to set aside many of the fruits of their labours to guard against future misfortune. Such luck could not hold forever, and not long after that happy year, three important changes occurred. Two of these three things were easily recognized by the people of Krannogberg as new Runecastings by Rulla. However, as oft is the case with important events, no one could have imagined the importance of the third event at the time it occurred.

As for the first important change, before the winter was out, Helgya took ill. Fevers gripped her and left her sweating in bed. Torga Danail and two other women who had learnt some healing from Helgya tended to the seeress but they could not defeat the spirit that attacked her. Magon came to her bedside and sat in a trance for an entire day. When he finally collapsed onto her dirt floor in a pool of sweat of his own, he croaked that he had done all he could, and that he did not believe it was enough.

However, Magon did not battle the disease spirit in vain; his struggle granted Helgya enough strength to wake the next morning. She spoke to the women around her but she made no sense. She spoke of devils obsessed with power, gems and other riches, and dragons coming to life. She railed against seas that bore no fish and barren hills that provided no fodder. She spoke of strange men in the settlement and a time of shield maidens. She spoke of rivers of blood and many other horrors.

Magon had slept by then and came to hear Helgya's ravings. He was too wise to dismiss them as such, but he instructed the women not to dwell on what they had heard, for nothing came in verse, as was Helgya's wont when she saw a possible future. Magon stayed at Helgya's bed throughout the day and listened to her. She gripped his arm often and stared at him through crazed eyes. Magon recognized the spirit of insanity that he had battled the day before in her eyes and he felt fear that he was perhaps in the presence of Sk'van. It spat nonsense at him until Helgya's spirit could win back control for a time. Eventually the words took better form but conveyed the same bedevilled meanings. He prayed to Heligat to withdraw Her demon and to Guliveg to nurture Helgya's life.

Magon had already felt despair when a violent fit took hold of Helgya's body. She convulsed and writhed and screamed into the night. Finally she lay at rest gasping for breath. The crazed eyes of the madness spirit looked at Magon, but when Helgya spoke, she broke into verse. Her words brought back a glimmer of hope to the priest for she spoke of a grand future for the folk. Unlike her words after the birth of the four bairns, Helgya's words did not slip from her lips in whispers. Instead, she shrieked them to the rafters. Also unlike the ominous verse of the previous winter, with talk of "swans of death" - ravens - gorging on flesh and "a sorry clan on Jarlag ships," all could understand the hopeful message of this latest seeing: their settlement would give the Fjordlanders their first king.

Once the words had escaped her mouth, Helgya closed her eyes for the last time and died in peace. After Magon had prepared Helgya's soul for its voyage to Hondrig's weighing, he called in the women. He looked at them in silence for a long while before finally saying, "I know you have heard much from

Helgya's mouth this past day, and in particular her last vision. I shall not ask you to keep these words to yourselves. Indeed, I shall speak to Hondsar about calling a moot so that all can hear. I only wish to warn you that the ways of the spirits and the practices of the Gods are plagued with uncertainty. Sk'van is strong in the spirit world, and even benevolent spirits themselves would tell you that prophesies show but a possible future. We have heard tale of a king here this night. We know that other folk have kings to rule over them. Do we want one here? I understand they demand taxes under pain of death, they live lavishly, they favour their friends and only their friends. Perhaps having a king is no great thing.

"Also, who is to say that when this village produces a king that it will not be because someone betrays our trust in him, turns traitor to us and hands us all to a foreigner? Might Tanat the Rogue not call that producing a king?

"All I ask of you is this," Magon continued, "We have been given a glimmer of hope among words of doom. Think of it as a tiny flame in a gale. We must nurture the understanding of these words just as we pray to Guliveg to nurture the spark of life. We should not use them to fill ourselves with false pride. Nor should we share them with outsiders. Conduct yourselves with wisdom."

The women responded with enough silence that Magon thought perhaps his warning had achieved its desired effect. He left the women to tend to the body and walked out into the winter night. He had heard his share of strange visions from Helgya during her lifetime but none had seemed to hint at such profound events until the morning after the four babes had come into the world the year before. Not for the first time, he wondered whether the births of the four children were as fortunate as everyone thought. Magon wandered long and far through the snow that night and he did indeed decide to speak to Hondsar about calling a moot so that all the folk could consider the words.

Returning to the village during the first light of day, he saw a white owl fly among the trees of the Harrowood and snatch up a vole from the ground.

§

As Magon lamented Helgya's death with the Darnok chieftain Hondsar the next morn, the second important change occurred. He had voiced his disquiet over Helgya's vision when a warning horn echoed off the fjords. Hondsar hurried as fast as his old frame could manage to don his armour and grab his old claymore from above his hearth. He dispatched his wife, Yellik, to muster the children and lead them up to the plateau. Magon, too, ran to his cottage and readied himself for battle, as did all the men and women of fighting age in the settlement. Yellik and the Darnok children had not climbed far up the snowy slopes of the fjord when they saw the first longboat sail into view: the Sea Wolves had come early that year to collect their tithe.

Sleek, filled with strong, fierce warriors, the ships were a flurry of oars stroking the water in precise unison. Their sails were emblazoned with shapes of terror; horned demons wreathed in flame, lightning striking between two tall mountains rising from a dark sea, a rain of blood against a backdrop of burnt out roundhouses, and a scarlet dragon coiled around a huge, sickly green gem. All the longboats sported the same figurehead; a white, snarling wolf leaping forward from the prow. Three full longboats accompanied the leader, while another, with fewer men to pull the oars, rounded the headlands some distance behind. The Krannogbergers recognized them as the Arctic Wolves, one family of the Unsettled Clan, and they knew these Sea Wolves would want a tithe of new recruits to pull oars on that last ship.

The men of the village formed two ranks on the ice-caked, rocky shore and waited. Some prayed to Karn to grant Her blessing upon them should there be a fight. They did not have long to wait before the first longboat hung a shield from the mast - an announcement that they did not come to wield the fiery brand or to bloody their axes - and the folk expelled a deep breath in relief. The longboats glided among chunks of bobbing ice in the sound accompanied by the clatter of oars against gunnel. Despite the shield hung on the mast, when the boats finally thrust up onto the stony beach, the men who stepped ashore had weapons at their belts. The Sea Wolves were all manner of men; large and wide, small and lithe. But they all had muscles filling their shirt sleeves, they all sported long, braided beards and they stank of sweat, brine, and rotten fish.

While the Sea Wolves flooded the beach, a large man stepped forward and surveyed the villagers. He was squat but seemed hewn from stone rather than made of flesh. A long, braided moustache gave him a menacing look and added to his rough features. He nodded to the two ranks of men that had formed in defence of the village and announced, "You do well to meet as such; no Fjordlander should greet a threat by cowering behind the skirts of his women."

"You have little to teach us about being Fjordlanders, Kindron Sopallig," Leigh, young Cairn's father, replied. "We have all served the Sea Wolves and paid our *lifgyld*. We now live our lives as free folk; how they should be lived. But you would know none of that. You have never followed that path."

Kindron Sopallig laughed before responding, "Indeed, my old friend. I remember you revelling in our raids across the sea against the Lanace. You liked them because they never gave us a fight. They always tried to buy us off and you were just as happy when they did!" He laughed again and continued, "Well, I hope you have found peace now. Let me say I have no desire to disturb it. We're doing well and need not raze your squalid little village. No, we'll take our tithe and leave you to your goats."

"Kindron, even you must know the difference between goats and sheep," Leigh retorted.

Again the Sea Wolf laughed. "I'll leave you to the knowledge of sheep, Leigh," he said with a smirk and a wink. Then he turned to Hondsar and asked, "Do you still claim the chieftainship?" A shocked silence fell, only broken by the gentle waves washing across the stony beach; no one had expected a Sea Wolf to come ashore and claim leadership of the settlement.

After a moment, the old chief stepped forward and replied, "I do. Nothing I have seen here would cause me to leave behind my steading and head off into the hills. If you want my title, young man, then you shall have to take it from me."

For a third time the Sea Wolf laughed. "No, old man, I meant what I said to my friend Leigh. I have no desire to take up the husbandry of cattle and ... sheep. I shall harry the southerners' shores for a while yet. However, before you set your mind to getting yourself killed, you might want to take a look at Knab Sokilg there." The Sea Wolf gestured to the last, under-manned longboat that approached. At its prow stood a striking hulk of a man all decked out for war. A bushy black beard flowed over the gleaming metal chest plate worn by soldiers of the Empire far to the southeast. Sokilg's long dark locks of hair spilled from beneath a sturdy helm and his left arm clutched a target shield forged from steel in the shape of the head of a wolf. In his other hand he held a large double-bladed axe. The longboat glided to shore, its keel grinding onto the pebble beach. The warrior leapt down into the knee-deep water and strode ashore. He marched up to Kindron Sopallig and bowed his head, one last time. Kindron initiated the Freedom Rite by ordering, "Say the words."

Knab looked up. "I have paid you my *lifgyld*. My time among the Sea Wolves has ended."

Kindron nodded and replied:

The Sea Wolves release you. You have served well.
Hold our wrath in your mind, for you will need its
strength in times of strife.

Hold our courage in your heart, for you will need its
power in times of darkness.
Hold not your home against us, for you will need us
in times of war.

Then he slapped the man on the biceps, pointed to Hondsar and said, "There's your man. He's a greybeard. I wouldn't take his rule from him if I were you. I recall the great, erstwhile Timber Wolf captain, Tülig Sodag, saying that all his best raids were planned by Hondsar here. They had so much success that he paid off his *lifgyld* in four years."

"No," Knab stated. "I am ill-forged to be a crofter, a herder or a fisher. I shall rule or I shall die."

Hondsar stepped forward, nodded, and asked, "I must know something. Why have you come here, of all places?"

"We have heard that your collection of cottages has done well of late. If I am to adapt to a life of ease, I may as well do it in a place of wealth."

Finally Hondsar's turn came to laugh, spilling the vapour of his breath into the winter day, "You'll find no life of ease here. I am not a stupid man; I have no doubt that you will take my title from me. However, these people shall make you earn your right to keep it. Also, remember the price of success and look for that courage Kindron spoke of when, in years to come, you feel your joints ache every time the Tears of the Ghosts fall. Come then," Hondsar ordered. "There's no point in putting this off."

Knab shook his head and said, "Your pride is touching, old man. But I have no wish to kill you. Walk off. The next village will welcome your wisdom."

"It was never my *wyrd* to balk in the face of challenges," Hondsar replied. "Do not insult me by taking false pity on me now." The giant Sea Wolf shrugged and stepped forward. He swung his axe in a great sweep. Hondsar met it with his shield but the blow hurled him to the icy ground. Knab closed on the prone chief and heaved the axe in a wide arc from behind his back, over his head and down. Hondsar rolled aside but Knab altered his swing enough. The blade clove through armour, skin, and bone alike. Hondsar gave a final cry, writhed on the ground for a moment, and then slumped against the rocky shore.

Torga Danail, the healer, gave a cry and ran forward, though no one had any doubt that Hondsar had died. Many a villager held hands to gaping mouths in stunned silence. Others let out a deep breath and turned their attention to their new chieftain.

Kindron Sopallig stepped up and slapped Knab on the back. "There you have it," he observed. "You've finally got your own command. Now, get me some replacements from among your new clan."

§

The whole village grieved - they had lost Helgya and Hondsar on consecutive days - and so the following day again was given over to commemorating their lives. Kindron had the Arctic Wolves stay on for those observances, partly because of the reputation of old Hondsar, partly for the feasting that comes with any funeral. If Knab or the others in his new clan objected to the Sea Wolf presence, no one voiced their displeasure. Magon led the townsfolk and the Sea Wolves through the snows up to the Harrowood, to the town's newest burial cairns. Then, despite the bitter cold brought on the winter wind, he sang the *Cleaving Rite* in its entirety, all one hundred and one verses. Only the eldest villagers knew it well enough to sing along with him, and none of the Sea Wolves, but everyone knew the refrain and their voices made it come to life:

Hondrig,
> *Master of the Deciding,*

Hondrig,
> *to Your shores a soul now sails.*

Master,
> *when You do the Weighing,*

Master,
> *let our love touch the scales.*

Hondrig,
> *as You bid us so we live,*

Hondrig,
> *waves, reefs, sleet and gales.*

Master,
> *weights of mercy You can give,*

Master,
> *let our grief touch the scales.*

Knab stood at Magon's side through the rite, his head bowed in respect, a gesture that the Darnok did not anticipate, but that they appreciated. When Magon completed his singing, then Knab did another thing that the Krannogbergers did not foresee, he approached Yellik, Hondsar's widow, dropped to one knee and presented her a bag of coin. "This be *weregyld* for your loss."

Expressions of surprise took hold of the visages of the watching Darnok and genuine shock appeared on that of the Arctic Wolves' leader Kindron. *Weregyld* was part of the tradition of payments upon causing a person's death or for maiming another, under pain of being declared an outlaw should payment not be made. The tradition spelled out specific weights of silver that needed paying dictated by the rank of the person and by the nature of the maiming or death; so much for the death of a herder, so much for the loss of a hand of a member of a village council, so much for the drowning of a seeress. Challenging a chieftain for rule did not require such a payment, therefore the offer of *weregyld* took most onlookers by surprise, but Yellik's face revealed more anger than bereavement. She looked down on Knab and considered the size of the bag. "If it be *weregyld*, Hondsar was too old to be worth a bag so big," she declared. "If it be to take his place in my heart, Hondsar was too good a man to be worth a bag so small."

"No bag would be big enough."

"No. Right enough."

"Consider it, then, *lifgyld* for the settlement, for the loss of their chieftain and for that of the wise woman of whom Leigh spoke to me. Let it bring something of benefit for those losses."

"In my time, I was a shield wench to Hondsar. I saw him take the chieftainship here from Jurgin Sokrillan. I know the way of our folk. To claim your authority here, you do not need my goodwill, something you shall never buy."

"No, indeed I do not. But you could do great deeds with a chieftain's *lifgyld*. It strikes me as wise to allow you to do so. Take it. Do some good with it."

Yellik nodded, took the bag from Knab's hand and the villagers considered it a good sign.

Chapter Two

After the dead had been laid to rest, the Sea Wolves demanded their tithe. They accepted half a hull-full of grain and a barrel of salted meat as well as one youth they deemed of fighting age in spite of the protests of his father that he was but fourteen. Heavier tithes were not uncommon, but Knab taking the chieftainship had changed things. Everyone knew the new Darnok leader could have prevented a heavier tithe; in addition to Krannogberg's existing strength of arms, Knab brought with him three other warriors who mustered out at the same time, and two of those men had capable axe wenches who joined them. With new warriors in their ranks, the settlement could have caused the Sea Wolves too much misery had they demanded too great a tithe. Also, the considerable payment of *lifgyld* from those who mustered out placated the Arctic Wolves; they could acquire stores they required without bloodshed, be it horsehair for mending ropes or driving between a ship's strakes, wool for sails, foodstuffs, iron axe heads, or planks for effecting ship repairs.

Two others also joined the Darnok during that Sea Wolf visit; their bard and a Straeling woman who was wife to one of the warriors Knab brought ashore with him. The Straeling stood shorter than most Fjordlander women, had quick eyes, and dark ringlets that spilled around her face rather than being tied into orderly braids. Thay's mother, Thülla, elbowed her husband, Rig, when the latter's eyes lingered too long on that spill of hair. She stayed close to her husband, Gunder Sohargar, but otherwise showed no sign of worry about her new clan.

All through the spring, Knab displayed his mettle to the villagers. He did not take Hondsar's home as was his right. Instead, he let Yellik remain in her cottage, accepted Leigh and Fallig's invitation to stay with them for the remainder of the winter, and he set about building himself a steading. Despite paying out his *lifgyld* to the Sea Wolves and *weregyld* to Yellik, his wealth remained substantial, and so he hired the best builders in the settlement to help him. He even brought in some from Narhaven, the next village up the coast, and before the beginning of summer, the village featured four new cottages. Contrary to his banter the day he arrived, he was no layabout; he worked relentlessly from dawn to dusk, until the long length of summer days and short hours of night made such labour too exhausting even for a man of Knab's qualities.

When he had his home built - a modest cottage set back from the strand whose only extravagance was a covered porch at the front where he could sit on a bench protected from whatever might fall from the Godspace and look at the water. He walked the villagers' summer ranges as soon as the snows allowed it. He visited every mountain lodge, spoke to every person under his charge, and assessed every defence. The rest of the clan watched Knab carefully, warily appraising their new chieftain, and they nodded approval to each other at these displays of concern for the Darnok's well-being.

Before spring turned to summer, Knab brought the best shipwrights to the settlement. Together they agreed upon a design and built a longboat the likes of which had never been seen before. Like other longboats, it was sleek, but it was longer by a score of spans, making it quicker than other Fjordlander vessels. It featured other innovations, a tiny cabin for its captain at the rear and a cramped sleeping quarters below decks where some of the crew not on the oars could lie down. When Knab launched it into the reach, he declared to the villagers, "I grew to love the Sea Wolves as brothers, but Hondrig damn me if I'll have my folk rely upon them for my very life in a time of strife."

He named the vessel *Wyrdforger* and felt his breast swell with pride when he looked upon it. Before the autumn set in, he took delegations to visit neighbouring settlements, not just to recruit workmen, but to establish good relations with their chieftains.

Knab was not alone in displaying his mettle to the Darnok. That day after Knab's accession to the chieftainship, the Sea Wolf bard, a man called Kyre Sobelden, paid his *lifgyld* and stayed in Krannogberg under odd circumstances. He hadn't intended to muster out of the Sea Wolves, but the evening after Hondsar's funeral feast he had a strange dream. At the time he told no one of what the dream revealed, but it nevertheless prompted him to hand over a gold armband to Kindron and stay with the Darnok.

Kyre was a tall, dark-haired man with bright eyes of green and lips ever shaped into an ironic smile. He was known more for his skill with harp and woman than with axe or sword; instead of having bulging muscles and a thirst for blood, he had nimble fingers and a thirst for mead. Although he mustered out with only his harp as an instrument, he was also skilled with the flute and fiddle, instruments he somehow managed to obtain within a moon of setting foot ashore. His beard wouldn't grow bushy, so he kept it trim and narrow, revealing the high cheekbones on his mischievous face as well as a long, narrow neck. He became the village's first bard in a generation.

Kyre had a taste for intricate melodies, well-suited to his fleet fingers, and he played many a complex ballad late into the night. However, he could turn his harp into a thumping drum, tapping his fingers on its wood or slapping the thicker strings with his hand, percussion that would accompany his baritone voice when chanting the old sagas. He would also take his bow and craft more raucous sounds when the mood of the round-house or the particular moment in a saga demanded it. He had a natural understanding of how music beguiled its listeners, and knew enough to eschew the melodic intricacies he so loved and to keep a lament pure and simple. He could even set people dancing with jigs, no mean feat on a harp.

The Darnok quickly took Kyre into their hearts and into their homes. He devoted himself to learning the local lore and setting it to verse. The folk approved of this, though they enjoyed even more his songs of feats of renown won by Fjordlanders - usually Sea Wolves - on far-flung shores. They lost themselves in such sagas, transported from their village clear across the Boldring Mountains or through the Demon's Teeth to exotic lands that learnt to fear the axe and the chieftain's claymore.

Kyre followed Knab on the new chieftain's visits to the summer ranges and he composed songs to celebrate the stunning beauty of the rugged mountains, the wind-swept plateau, and the majestic sweep of the fjords down to the sea. When Knab busied himself in town, Kyre would walk the ranges himself and stay with the herding folk on the plateau. By the time the autumn gales arrived and the herders returned to Krannogberg, it finally dawned on the villagers that Kyre had not yet even built a home. Every Darnok spent the two days after Hearthfire celebrations raising a cottage for the bard in record time, with Kyre playing them tunes all the while. Only old Magon detected a bittersweet tone to the songs and he realized the bard enjoyed ranging and staying each night with different folk. Indeed, many of the Darnok felt a tug of regret with the completion of that cottage and soon urged Kyre to resume his past ranging, cottage or no.

Knab also took the bard with him whenever he visited the neighbouring clans, for a song could, at times, thaw a man's heart when no spoken word could. The village bairns begged Kyre to tell them tales of adventure and horror. His accounts of Fjordlander legends were sometimes too vivid for the children and they would lie awake at night in terror after a harrowing tale. He spent long evenings with Magon and soon had many of the Tales of the Godspace put to music.

Kyre made the village come to life with his lore, his songs, and his odd taste for life. The Darnok awoke one winter morning, with flurries floating down from the Godspace, to see - and hear - Kyre lying on his back, naked as the day he was born, at the prow of a dory floating off shore, his harp in his hands and a song on his lips, trying to find the perfect rhyme for "mackerel." He found he could get all the village curs, particularly Rolf, to howl like wolves if he plucked his harp just so.

He had been an oar mate of Knab for many years and, thus, people watched them carefully when they were together, looking for cues as to how to act with the new chieftain. Whether or not Kyre's playful spirit drove him, or whether he perceived fear and uncertainty through the show of detached reserve among the clan and felt compelled to dispel it, his repertoire included light interludes mockingly glorifying Knab's plans;

The chieftain walks the Darnok lands
 and thinks about the raiding bands
that surely lurk on Hondrig's Bight
 and test the Darnok will to fight.

If battle comes to Darnok lands
 and ships arrive upon the strand,
where shall the stoutest swing the axe?
 Where shall the Jarlags feel those whacks?

He marches to, he marches fro,
 the Darnok need a place to go.

The chieftain builds a fortress strong,
 six feet tall and four feet long,
A redoubt which the folk approve;
 a pit, should someone's bowels move.

He no more marches to and fro,
 the Darnok have a place to go.

The folk listened and watched. Knab never fell into a rage at Kyre's parodies. He might shake his head in resigned desperation, he might toss chunk of bread at the bard, or he might even let loose a blast of laughter, but he did not become cruel or violent. The Darnok came to realize that they need not fear Knab and they opened their hearts to him.

Word spread up and down the coast about the bard's talent. Boats would sail down from Narhaven on Gods' Days just to hear Kyre sing and play. Magon and the other villagers soon thought highly of the newcomer and, although they missed Hondsar, they all knew that the visit of the Sea Wolves that year could have turned out much, much worse.

They did not know at the time that Kyre's decision to stay in Krannogberg represented the third important change. No one would until much, much later.

§

As soon as the herders had brought their beasts down from the hills, Knab called a moot. He set before the folk a plan of practical measures they could take to defend themselves better, either from attack by the Sea Wolves, or by other Fjordlander clans, particularly their old enemies the Jarlags. He listened well to sound arguments and showed flexibility in the building of his designs, the majority of which in that first year centred around thorough training for fighting in a shield wall. This was all new to the Darnok, for Hondsar had never seemed to like change, though Uilig, Lora's father, said that what the old chieftain really had never liked was the sharing of silver that invariably came with new ideas.

Despite the cautions voiced by the moot about the Jarlags, Knab decided to go and speak to the rival chieftain down the coast. He sailed *Wyrdforger* and took with him two smaller boats filled with warriors. Even so, he took care to hang a shield from his flagship's mast and to make his way slowly up Caljürd's Arm. The reception that they received surprised all the men of Krannogberg except their new chieftain. No watch fires blazed, no warning horns sounded, and no boats sought to intercept them. The men of Sangspit did form ranks to greet their ancient rivals from the north, but they did not seek to start any trouble.

Knab came ashore in much the same manner as he had six moons before in Krannogberg. He looked impressive in his Chayan Empire breastplate, but he did not take his axe in hand. The Jarlags' chieftain, Rigald Sokaroth, stepped forward, hand on the hilt of his claymore, and said, "I see your mast shield." Sokaroth, raven haired and covered in scars, stood as tall as Knab but did not carry the new chieftain's bulk. Even so, no one doubted the tales that they had heard of his deadliness, for his dark eyes flashed with danger and he moved with a fluid quickness.

Knab smiled from behind his bushy, black beard and replied, "I knew I could count on you, Rigald, not to shoot flaming arrows into the hull of my new boat. You have my thanks."

The other chieftain frowned and said, "I may yet. Why in Skalagg did you wash ashore with the Darnok? I would have made you welcome here."

"I doubt it, my friend," Knab replied. "I did not have much taste for becoming a vassal to anyone after so many years of serving that bastard Kindron."

"He drives men no harder than any other Sea Wolf chieftain," the Jarlag chief declared.

Knab shrugged, "Perhaps not, but I still have the right to hate him. I have taken the chieftainship of the Darnok."

Rigald Sokaroth huffed at that. "And now you want to sort some things out. I'll clear out the roundhouse. Your new people can stay there while you and I talk. I hope they brought their own food, for our stores cannot feed the likes of them."

If Knab took offence at the poor hospitality, he did not let it show. Indeed, for all the time that he ruled as chieftain, neither his own folk nor any outsider would ever learn to read the thoughts behind his neutral expression. Instead he nodded and replied, "Can you place a guard upon them? I'd hate for someone with a feud to feed to take this opportunity to cause trouble."

Sokaroth nodded and gestured to the surrounding fjord. "Let us go up there together, alone, and talk."

Only a glance back at Kyre in *Wyrdforger* hinted that Knab might hold some misgiving at treating with Sokaroth alone.

All afternoon the Darnok waited in the Jarlag roundhouse. They kept men posted at all windows and many paced to and fro in the house's cramped confines. At the end of the afternoon, just as dusk fell on Sangspit, the two men returned and everyone could see the discussion had not gone well. The men of Krannogberg came forth from the roundhouse to meet their leader. Many a Jarlag, who had been brooding in the town, also came forward to stand with their chieftain. Thus, a great many people heard the end of the conversation between the two chieftains.

"Rid yourself of that boat or we will rid you of it ourselves," Sokaroth menaced. "We will have watchers. The next time we see it in these waters, we expect Sea Wolves to crew it."

Knab glared at the Jarlag chieftain and stated, "Keep watch then. Watch as we prosper. Watch as we grow strong. Watch as best you can. You may learn something." With that, he loaded up his men into the boats and set sail for home. The trip was a sombre one.

§

The Jarlags came in the deep of winter, before dawn on a bitterly cold night not a week before the four toddlers turned two. Three Jarlag longboats filled with men plied the risky winter seas. The Darnok shared a watchtower atop Hargur's Head with the Yareg clan of Narhaven so they should have had warning of the approach of the strange vessels. But the youngsters in the watchtower were huddled out of the winter wind behind the stone wall, dozing fitfully, and didn't keep watch from the arrow slit facing west onto Hondrig's Bight. The vessels didn't veer north to Narhaven. Instead, they crossed to the Andersfjord as quickly as the strong wind would take them, driving chunks of ice out of their way. They rowed past Hargur's Head and bore down on Krannogberg, driven forward by the fierce west wind and the swells funnelling in from the Bight.

The captains of the vessels had not hung their shields from the masts.

Rolf, who heard the thud of a hull against ice, gave the first warning, baying into the night. Krannogberg's other dogs joined in, not needing to know the cause of their sudden distress to lend their voices to the warning. Soon the entire village was awake, reaching for their armour and their weapons. Rolf saw the ships emerge from the dawn mist and his bark changed from a low, thumping warning to a quick ear-shattering staccato. When the keel of the first longboat scraped on the ice-encrusted gravel beach, Rigald Sokaroth leapt first to the ground as was fitting for a clan chieftain. He scrambled after the pack of barking dogs, Rolf at its head, and dispersed them. His clansmen followed, pouring over the gunnels and skittering their way up the gravel slope to the head of the beach.

Odman Sostig's home was the closest to where the first boat landed. Rigald made for the cottage door, but though the dogs scattered from his initial attack, a few of the boldest came from behind at his ankles, forcing him to spin around to defend himself. They finally retreated as three Jarlags sprang at them, swinging their axes. The delay was enough to give Odman the time he needed to get his wife and daughters out the back door an instant before Sokaroth kicked in the front. The light wasn't good enough for Odman to recognize the tall, scar-ridden chieftain as the intruder, but he would have met whatever attacker in exactly the same manner, swinging his axe and throwing his body into the breach of the doorway. Alas, the space restricted the swing of an axe, and all Sokaroth had to do was turn the point of his claymore towards the charging form. The big sword caught Odman in the shoulder and bit deeply, forcing a cry of agony from his lips. But the sword couldn't halt Odman's momentum and the man knocked Sokaroth back into the threshold, blocking the way of his clansmen. Odman struck at Sokaroth's face with the butt of his axe, but the chieftain was too quick and ducked back, wrenching free his sword from the defender's shoulder.

Odman held the doorway for a few more moments as the Jarlags flooded around his cottage. He never knew it, but holding up the enemy chieftain prevented Sokaroth from organizing the decisive attack he hoped would net him slave women and children, riches, the finest longboat in Fjordland, and the fame of having finally vanquished their rivals. For when Sokaroth burst from the cottage's back door, a flaming brand in his hand, he was met by a shield wall of fifty men and sixteen women anchored by a black-bearded mass in a helm and a foreign breastplate.

Sokaroth knew his attack needed surprise and panic. With his men running amok, he had no chance of pulling them into the organized attack he would need to break a shield wall. He knew without taking a moment to think that he couldn't defeat Knab Sokilg's defence. But his clansmen had one thing the Darnok did not at that moment; mobility. He brandished his flaming torch and taunted Knab, "So, chieftain, can a man who can't protect his people's homes truly claim such a title?" He threw the brand high into the pre-dawn murk. It cast a blazing streak through the air and landed with an explosion of sparks on the dried out shingles of the roof of the roundhouse that the shield wall defended. The shingles smouldered in the wind, threatening to catch fire. "You've a problem there to solve!" Sokaroth yelled, retreating into Odman's cottage.

The terror of the night attack was one of Cairn's first memories. It would always come to him in pieces: his mother, Fallig, holding him tight in the roundhouse, behind a target shield, herself holding a dirk the length of her forearm; the screams of panicked children; the wailing of his friends as they reacted to the fear that smothered them. He also remembered Loska, Lora's mother, shouting orders. He remembered screaming, himself, when a big man burst over the women's shield wall, grin on his face and death in his eyes. He remembered his mother striking out and the man's death wail adding to the clamour of the night.

Cairn also remembered the flames; those atop the roundhouse roof that forced the women to rip off swaths of its cedar shingles before the whole place burst into an inferno; those of the other cottages set alight by the Jarlags; those of the Darnok ships hauled up on land. He would always remember looking north along the strand and watching the huge, flowering blaze rising from *Wyrdforger*, illuminating the winter night.

The people of Krannogberg saw a different Knab once he was certain the apparent disorderly attack was no ruse to have the Darnok break up their shield wall. By that time the bulk of the fires had been set and the Jarlags were retreating to their longboats. Four, though, emerged from a cottage near the strand, one clasping the head of old Yellik by the hair and swinging it in circles. The others had much of old Hondsar's loot in their arms and they laughed as they jogged in pursuit of their retreating clansmen. The first of the Jarlag longboats was already back on the water and men were heaving the second boat into the fjord. Knab let forth a twisted cry that seemed to burst from the pits of Skalagg. He ran towards the four men on the beach, but he never would have intercepted them if not for the final heroics of Rolf. The shaggy dog darted out from behind a lobster trap and latched onto the first man's heel. The one swinging Yellik's head pitched forward in confusion. Another man tripped over his colleague while a third tripped over Rolf. The delay was enough for Knab.

The Krannogbergers saw one man burst upon four in a fury of arching axe sweeps. The last man, still on his feet, leapt away from the attack but misjudged the considerable length of Knab's reach. Knab's first attack struck him in the chest and the axe would have remained embedded there were it not for the chieftain's strength and fluidity of movement. Before the man hit the gravel, the axe was diving down on the next man. The man with Yellik's head couldn't get to his feet because Rolf had clamped his jaws about his ankle and was tugging like a demon. Rolf's victim struggled with his target shield but he couldn't bring it up in time and three axe blows were enough to finish him off. By that time the last of the attackers had regained his feet, but Knab rained blow after blow against the man's shield until a sudden low sweep took the man's legs out from under him. The end came one swing of the axe later.

The Darnok scrambled from fighting the Jarlags to fighting fires. Only Knab and Kyre didn't join the effort. They stared out into the Andersfjord, watching as the longboats rowed west in the dawn light. Knab didn't build another ship like *Wyrdforger*, but he did build a hatred for the Jarlags, one that matched any hatred a born Darnok could muster.

The next day, Tears of the Ghosts fell from the Godspace as if mourning the loss of ten Krannogbergers. Rigald Sokaroth's attack also destroyed two longboats and six fishing vessels in addition to Knab's flagship. Four cottages had burnt to the ground, though the folk saved the roundhouse.

§

The Darnok were not content to remain the victims of the raiding of the Sea Wolves or the Jarlags. They launched their first raid under Knab late in the winter, before the warmer air of spring cleared the snow from the high plains. The men of Krannogberg made a show for several days of preparing their remaining longboats, four older vessels that hadn't seen harsher action than a summer jaunt in many a year. They scraped barnacles, they replaced planks suspected of rot, they drove tarred horsehair between the strakes to prevent leaks, they replaced the masts and inspected the sails. They sailed on winter's last neap tide, on a clear, starry evening. They went out into the Bight, arriving at Sagear's Cove on Langsand Island early the next day, shields hung on their masts.

They spent until midday trading and visiting their Higgersuld clan neighbours under a rare azure winter sky. Their welcome was suiting from a friendly clan, and the people of Sagear's Cove gave them a dinner of herring and leeks in return for news of the Jarlag raid earlier that winter. Then Knab led a handful of the men up to the nearby shrine to Asgear, God of the Waves. The path to the shrine led past the centre of the island and then up a steep slope to a cairn upon a hilltop that looked out over the unending, undulating expanse of ocean glinting with blinding brilliance in the afternoon sun. A priestess emerged from a cottage just beneath the lip of the hill on the down-slope that led to a gravel beach that was the westernmost point of all Fjordland. She was young and spry and took no time climbing up the path to greet the visitors. She set down an earthen jug of sea water and a piece of driftwood and then clasped the hands of all those who had come to receive the blessing of Asgear, seeking their names and giving them hers.

She performed the *Rite of Wayfaring*, chanting rhythmically. As she chanted, she rocked back and forth with the jug in her hands, spilling the sea water onto the piece of driftwood at her feet. Her song was powerful, like the sea, and she sang it lustily:

Mover of the surf,
  who dwells within the deep,
from here upon the earth,

Your blessing we now seek,
 for these our sons,
 for these brave ones,
who dip their oars in your domain.

Mover of the waves,
 lie contented in the deep.
Modest gifts they crave,
 Your own good sleep,
  safe wayfarings,
  true, sound bearings,
 oh! See them safely home again.

Master of the tides,
 Sculptor of the seas,
Upon Your waves will ride,
 doers of great deeds.
  Guide their tall prows,
  bring them renown,
 let their last breath sing Your acclaim.

When she was done, Knab knelt before her and gave her a gleaming gold armband. The priestess took it and said, "This is a rich offering, Knab Sokilg."

"Asgear, and his priestess, have given the blessing I sought. I am grateful."

"The colour of the band does not guarantee you a safe journey. It may yet please the God of the Waves to have you join Him at His table to hear you tell your tales."

"I've merry tales to tell, 'tis true. But no, the colour of the band might be more important to the God's priestess, that she might pray more often and more vigorously on our behalf. Besides," he added, "the Gods have been generous with me, I should not be a miser in return."

The priestess nodded, slipped the armband over her wrist, and bade them goodbye. As they turned to walk back to Sagear's Cove, Rig Sowulf, Thay's father, fell in beside Knab and said, rather than asked, "You received the blessing you sought."

"I did."

"Would it have been the priestess' rite, or the sight from this here hill of yon longboat rowing like mad for the south?"

Knab slapped Rig on the back as they watched the Jarlag ship in the distance and he smiled. "I sussed out a thing or two on my sailings, Rig. Say your prayers with open eyes."

§

Rig understood more following that conversation: the oddness of extensive but visible preparations; sailing out of Krannogberg under a clear, starry night; the stop in Sagear's Cove when he would have driven south with all the speed he could muster out of his oarsmen. He also understood why Leigh and many of the other men who knew the high pastures had stayed behind in Krannogberg: the oddness of leaving behind capable men was less odd if they had their own tasks to perform. He looked at other things anew, namely the work Knab had started on a cabin up on the plateau after midwinter, an odd time to begin such a project. Groups of men carting lumber and rope up to the pasture on poor weather days could perhaps permit other things; Rig knew that from the southern-most curve of the Andersfjord to the northern-most reach of Caljürd's Arm was barely twelve leagues, a distance that men of the high pastures could cover if they were well-equipped, with snowshoes, hard tack, furs, and chunks of coal to get a fire going at need.

He was not surprised, then, when Knab put in that night at Jorrumsfjord, the struggling village of the Darnalths, close kin of the Darnok. Knab traded, at near a loss, the goods that he had procured in Sagear's Cove, but Rig understood. The message to the clansmen was clear; Jorrumsfjord had once suffered one of the most brutal raids ever inflicted by one clan upon another. A dozen years before, the Jarlags had come and killed every man they had found, raped and stolen most of the women, and rounded up the children. Only those out fishing or up on the hills with their herds had escaped. It was said that the young children had been given to Jarlag families but that the older ones, those who would remember their clan and perhaps one day take revenge on those who had ravaged them, had been sold as slaves to the Veneg, a backwards people who lived over the Boldring Mountains. The message Knab sent to the speedy longboat that had started shadowing their movements out to sea was equally clear; the Darnok were working themselves up for a fight.

Rig had grown up in Spearberg, just up the coast from the entrance to Caljürd's Arm, and had mustered out of the Sea Wolves to join the Darnok because he had met a spirited young Krannogberger, Thülla, during a stay in Narhaven. Still, he never forgot the waters of his home down the coast and he knew why the Jarlags had prospered so well, protected as they were behind the shoals, reefs, jutting headlands, and rampant currents where the arm met the sea. Putting the other clues together, then, he was not surprised to see that shadowing longboat run on the wind before them the next day and round the headlands into Caljürd's Arm well ahead of the Darnok fleet. Neither was he surprised when Knab led the fleet in a broad curving sweep out to sea, well away from the headlands. The Jarlag fleet lay at anchor beyond the breakers surging above the reef that closed half the entrance. Smaller objects, too small to be boats, floated off the headland, and Rig guessed they were banks of barrels holding a surprise for attackers, or perhaps holding something as simple as a chain suspended in the water just below the surface, something that would create drag on any attacking longboats.

Knab brought the fleet about, tacking and re-tacking to hold his place in front of Caljürd's Arm. In the waning of the afternoon, he finally hung his shield from the mast of his vessel and approached the Jarlags. He brought his ship to within hailing distance and stood at the bow, dangling forward over the waves, hanging from the glowering bear head set upon the prow. Rig was in that ship and he heard the hatred in the banter tossed between Knab and his Jarlag rival, Rigald Sokaroth. Knab snarled at Sokaroth that the Jarlags had no honour, Sokaroth taunted that Knab's folk should have the courage of their convictions and come and fight. The taunts went on for longer than Rig thought necessary if Knab wanted to work the Darnok warriors into a seething frenzy, but then he spotted the finger of black smoke rising into the sky far to the east, deep up Caljürd's Arm and suddenly Knab's tone changed.

"I leave you now to think on your dishonour, Rigald," he yelled with a smile and a wave.

"Think on your own as you row home with your tails between your legs, coward. Think on the embarrassment you have suffered in front of your men. Knab the fearful! Knab the weak! Knab the failure! The man who should not lead!"

"I'll take your advice to heart, Rigald. Insults from a man who forgets his home has a back door." Knab pointed over the heads of the Jarlags. "I've an inkling of the trouble that awaits you when you get back home. Remember when the hunger bites this year, pay full *weregyld* to the Jorrumsfjorders and we might even help you stave off starvation!"

With that he jumped down from the prow of his ship and ordered a tack north, upwind, to take them home.

Rig and his oar mates marvelled at Knab's cunning when they returned home; savage reprisal for the attack that had killed ten Darnok earlier that winter. The real raiding party led by Loska crossed over the snow-clad plateau later the same night of the neap tide. Each pair of Darnok dragged a sled behind them laden with the materials they had stored on the heights. Rolf and some other village dogs used to the work dragged the hull of a fishing boat, to which the Darnok had fastened skids, making a sled of it. They encountered no resistance, no alarm. They clambered down to the northern end of Caljürd's Arm and spent a night reassembling the boat, attaching its benches, fixing its lines. The next day they had sailed into Sangspit unopposed and unheralded. There was an initial fight when they started breaking into homes and rounding up the women and children; some of the women were shield wenches and some of the older men left behind by Rigald Sokaroth were not so old. Twelve dead Jarlags convinced the others to cease their resistance, though many fled.

The Darnok herded the villagers into the roundhouse and then went through the remaining buildings, taking everything of wealth and splashing whale oil everywhere. They forced young boys to drive the herds of cattle and sheep out into the snowy pastures, and then they set every building ablaze. To show their moral superiority over those who had acted so viciously in Jorrumsfjord, they allowed the Jarlags to leave the roundhouse before setting it alight. Then they took five of the prettiest young women, boarded the fishing boat, and left with their loot.

They returned home with enough gold to pay *lífgyld* to the families of Odman Sostig and the other Darnok who lost their lives in the Jarlag attack. Enough was left over for Knab to consider building stone defences for the town. The grimness of the Darnok mood that winter lifted with the raid's success as they gloated in their revenge. Three of the young Jarlag women even accepted Darnok husbands. The other two were given over in tithe to the Sea Wolves on their next visit.

Kyre composed songs about the raid that the Darnok sang for years upon years.

Chapter Three

During that fateful winter of raids and upheaval, the four youngsters spoke their first words, took their first steps, and grew quickly. Cairn's size outstripped the others', although Thay stood taller, while Lora and Lars both moved with such speed that their parents learnt to keep a close eye on them. Little events of daily life hinted at the babies' nascent personalities. Cairn was jolly but his temper tantrums surpassed anything the others could muster. Lora enjoyed learning almost as much as showing off her new-found knowledge. Lars showed a stubborn streak and he took longer to heed the word "no," while Thay was quiet but showed great curiosity.

By the time the following spring rolled around, and the time came for Leigh and Fallig to take Cairn up to the summer ranges again, their burly little boy flew into one of his rages at the prospect of leaving his friends. The other three also protested Cairn's departure for the summer. These protests became an annual rite of spring sure as the sighting of the first wryneck or the first flush of emerald on the plateau above the fjords.

As the years passed, the village folk slowly came to know each child for the individual he or she was rather than just as part of a gaggle.

Cairn remained heavy-set and dark. His black hair and his brown eyes masked a mirth that bubbled in him continuously. And yet, he remained the one of the four that people were least eager to anger. One winter day, Gelbrand Soingolf - a good three years older than the four bairns - used his fists to show Lars what he thought about the latter's bragging about having a special *wyrd*. Gelbrand suddenly found himself set upon by an enraged Cairn wielding a broom handle. All the village bairns learnt a lesson that day about Cairn's loyalty to his friends. However, he liked his luxuries and was ill-inclined to hard work. Lars joked that this laziness came from having the sole worry of lying on the ground dozing all day while the family's dogs did the hard work of looking after the livestock. Cairn laughed when Lars poked fun at him in this way, but Hondrig Himself had to defend anyone else who deliberately insulted Cairn, his family or his friends. And yet, for those who fell afoul of the young lad, a quick penance was always enough to have Cairn forget whatever slight had occurred. He remained his parents' only child.

Lora had a keen intellect to go with her auburn hair and flecked blue eyes. Only Thay could keep up with her when she began to piece together the clues to some childhood puzzle. Indeed, of all the youngsters in the village, only she and Thay spent time with Aganas, the wife of Gunder Sohargar, who still eschewed braids and let her dark ringlets spill around her head. Lora demonstrated great skill in picking up strange, Straelish words, just as other insights came more quickly to her than they did to many others. She refused to be separated from the boys when they fought their heroic, if imaginary, battles against the Jarlags or some wild band of Sea Wolves. Her spirit burned fiercer than Cairn's rages, but it was a kindly spirit to those around her. She loved to nurture and see things grow. Nalone, her sister who had come along after two years, greatly annoyed her, but she took care of her sibling, as she did for Rugar and Henkal, born another two and five years later respectively. Some in the village hoped that she would develop into another Helgya for she seemed to have something of the Sight; a knack for being at the right place at the right time or for avoiding the right place at the wrong time.

Lars was a typical Fjordlander, with hair so blonde it bordered on white, and vivid, blue eyes. He grew tall, well-muscled, and handsome. He poked fun at everything and anyone, except the stories of his people, which he revered. He enjoyed the traditions that governed life in Krannogberg: the prayers to the Gods at Hearthfire; the singing on Darknight; the frolicking under the long summer dusk of Brightnight. While Thay and Lora spent time with Aganas learning words in Straelish, he spent hours on end with Kyre the Bard and learnt to recite the stories of all the great heroes of the Darnok. His favourite tales were of battles fought defending the folk from the mythical *tosk-hyr* of the forests - the tusk men who stole cattle or sheep and raided isolated cottages on the plateau, enslaving any Fjordlander they could. He would take the longest of the four to see the value in a new idea, but would then become its fiercest advocate. He accepted his life on his father's fishing boat, but he longed for the arrival - some day far in the murky future - of the Sea Wolves so that he could prove his worth as a warrior. He dreamt of returning home trailing songs of renown in battle and carrying chests of gold. He took his arms training seriously and even as a young boy he could swing an axe well. His common age with the others naturally made them fast friends and he preferred their company over that of his brother Magnas, born four years after him, or his sister Alvag, who was six years his junior.

Grey-eyed, tawny-haired Thay also dreamt. Indeed, many came to say he dreamt too much. First, he was prone to the daydreams of all young boys; like Lars, he dreamt of glory in battle, but he also dreamt of whatever caught his imagination. He would dream of delivering luck to his family, of a bout of summer weather in the depths of winter, of witnessing majestic parts of the world. He would begin a morning darning fishing nets and lose himself among their threads only to be woken from his reverie to find his task completed but with no memory of having done so. Daydreams such as these are the stuff of all children - and his sister, Ellena, a year and a half his elder, often scolded him for it - but Thay also had other dreams. In these other dreams, a giant worm with great ruby wings would reveal itself to Thay and peer into his grey eyes. Thay would stare, transfixed, while the creature passed messages into his very mind. And the messages? - vague images of balance, fate, sacrifice, and rest - or resolution, at least. These dreams came at night, but they did not trouble his sleep. Indeed, every time he had one, he would awake feeling comforted and refreshed. These dreams he came to name his crimson dreams, for the colour of the giant worm, but also for the warmth that the dreams evoked in him.

In short, except for Thay's crimson dreams, the children were just like children anywhere.

§

After that winter raid by the Jarlags, Knab convinced the clan to invest time and wealth - their time and his wealth - in the clan's defences. Once they had pledged him a tithe of labour and once Magon had sought Orgor the Crafter's blessing, Knab set the folk to the raising of an earthen embankment around the town. He paid workers from across the Bight to dig a ditch and heap the dirt onto the embankment. His silver also coaxed some of the folk to trade their fishing season for work on the project. Finally, he gave some small cuttings of silver to farmers willing to lug rocks from their fields to provide a hard shell for the embankment, slowly turning it into a wall with an earthen centre, and in so doing, improving both the defences and the fields.

He worried over the points that blocked line of sight from town to Hargur's Head, where the Andersfjord gave onto Hondrig's Bight and atop which sat the watchtower that the Darnok shared with the Yareg of Narhaven. Cooperation took the edge off the savagery of Sea Wolves; if the Sea Wolves wanted more than a simple tithe somewhere on the Bight, they had to get in and out quickly or risk other clans coming in behind to capture or burn their precious longboats. He walked the path up to that watchtower often and brooded, looking down on the water. When standing up there on the cliff, the wind buffeting him and sending the strands of his bushy black beard fluttering about his face, Knab often frowned, thinking that a wily Sea Wolf captain, if he slipped across the Bight without the watchers in the watchtower seeing, could sail close to shore behind the lips of the points giving little time for the mustering of a defence.

It was on one of these walks high up the slopes of the fjord, further west along the water from Krannogberg, that he noticed in the fjord wall a deep crack in the rock that gave way to a cave. The step outside the crack enjoyed a commanding view across to the other shore and down to the foot of the fjord. He turned the cave into both a redoubt and a safe haven. He put in a store of whale oil, rags, bows and arrows so that enemies that approached town might find fire arrows raining down upon them. He had half the stock of the town's food put into barrels or big earthen jars and stored at the back of the cave, along with blankets and furs. Knab even got Kyre the Bard to coax a family of notoriously savage wild cats to take up residence in the cave, a job that took a month of crooning with fingers on harp cords, with bow to fiddle, and with fish heads proffered. He succeeded in the end but proclaimed, "that was a hard crowd!" The cats dealt with rats in the cave, though they never let anyone near the stores without paying a toll of fish entrails.

Knab also appraised the existing system of signal fires on the plateau, fires that those herders who lived up above the fjord from spring until autumn would light upon spying the approach of strangers. These he judged adequate, but he formally gave to Leigh, Cairn's father, the responsibility of ensuring that all families knew their role and remained vigilant.

If anyone ever wondered whether such measures were truly necessary, the Jarlag attack the previous winter reminded them of the cost of a lack of readiness. Every year the Sea Wolves came, usually the Black Wolves, the Timber Wolves, or Kindron's Arctic Wolves, and Knab judged the defences. Did the watchtower that Krannogberg shared with Narhaven alert the towns? Did the warriors arm themselves quickly and make a shield wall? Did the older folk get the children up to the redoubt quickly enough?

The Jarlags twice tested Krannogberg's defences and both times they retreated without bloodshed. The first time they came, forty of them tried Knab's trick of coming overland, but they did so when many Darnok were up on the plateau with their herds. The Jarlags closed in on the Andersfjord only to find a solitary Knab in the middle of the path leading down to town. Knab sat whistling on a chair that would not have been amiss in a dining hall and he carved a piece of driftwood with his dirk. When Rigald Sokaroth strode close, Knab looked up and said "bows."

"Bows?" Sokaroth echoed.

"Yes, Rigald, bows." Knab waited through the silence and then added, "Well, if you haven't sussed it out yet, it's the answer to the question in your men's minds."

"The question in my men's minds? Are you some sort of seer now, Knab? Or did the summer heat rot your brain?" Despite the boldness of Sokaroth's reply, many of the Jarlags cast their eyes about them in worry.

Knab laughed as he whittled shavings of wood onto his lap. "We've had a good summer, right enough. Good harvest. The livestock are plentiful and plump. The fishing's been bountiful, Asgear be blessed. Everyone's doing well.

"No, Rigald, the heat hasn't rotted my brain," Knab continued. "I just know that if I were an axe warrior up on this here plateau with you, I'd be wondering why my idiot of a chieftain hadn't ordered the fool in the chair cut down. And the answer, is bows."

"Bows?"

"Yes, Rigald, bows." Knab whistled and a hundred Darnok rose from the ground, casting aside blankets covered with grass and dirt, raising yew bows and fitting arrows to the bow strings. A dozen Darnok moved up behind Knab's chair, their aim trained on the leading Jarlag warriors. "Anyone lunges for me and they end up looking like a hedgehog. That's why you shouldn't order your men to cut me down. Get it? Bows.

"Now, we don't want the trouble of having to bury you or your men. If you turn around now, and I mean now Rigald, then you can go back the way you came and no one dies. If you want to test our bows, hesitate. It's your choice, Rigald, but the time to choose is now. Right now, Rigald. Choose."

Sokaroth chose. He turned his men back. The ring of Darnok separated to let the Jarlags pass. Once clear, Sokaroth called back many an insult, some of them inventive, but both sides knew who had come out on top.

§

The second Jarlag raid also had little direct effect on Krannogberg or the four children, now in their sixth year, but Knab recognized the cleverness in it nevertheless. Five Jarlag longboats entered the Bight one late afternoon and they bore down directly on the Andersfjord. The watchtower caught sight of them and raised the alarm. Krannogberg sprang to its defences as the horn in the watchtower sounded one long wail, one short blast, and a final long wail. The Jarlags were attacking Krannogberg. The old herded the young up to the redoubt, fire arrows were prepared, the Darnok's warriors took up their arms and came together at the town wall. Others prepared to tend to the wounded, or had hoes ready to pull shingles off cottages that might have their roofs set alight. They were ready, even Rolf, who stood with his hackles raised growling into the dusk.

Then notes of the horn changed to one long wail followed by three short blasts, sounding the warning for Narhaven, not Krannogberg. Knab ordered, "Ready the longboats!" As they were loading up their vessels, the horn blasted again, returning to the original warning. No sooner had they pulled the ships from the water and returned behind their wall when they heard the second alert again, the horn blaring the warning for Narhaven. Knab ordered Lora's mother, "Loska, take two quick rowers out in your crabber and find out what in Tanat's name is going on!"

They waited behind their defences as Loska took Thay's father, Rig, and Gunder Sohargar out onto the Andersfjord, rowing hard against the wind. The code changed again, signalling an attack on Krannogberg, but the little crabbing boat did not turn about and raise its sail. The Darnok stood at the defences as the horn returned again to one long note followed by three short ones. At length, Loska signalled to them and Rig ordered the longboats put in. No further horn blasts sounded as they headed out into the arm. Rounding Hargur's Head, they sighted the Jarlag fleet plying into the drawing night, heading southwest, towards the ocean with three Yareg longboats in tow.

When Darnok went ashore in Narhaven, they came in long after many other folk from around the Bight including the Ylfing out of from Dople, the Skolrüt from Ankvik, and the Skjöldung from Aldsund. Knab went to the village roundhouse and had to endure the anger of Anders Sologoth, chieftain of the Yareg. A great many of the common folk also looked upon the late arrival of the Darnok with cold, hard eyes as the chieftain railed, "Why'd you not come? Why'd you leave us to this fate?"

Knab held out his hands and replied, "The watchtower's horn blasts! They sounded the attack on Krannogberg!"

"They did no such thing!" spat Sologoth. "That was Rigald Sokaroth from the stern of his ship, that was! Were you so undone by a simple ruse, or were you craven?" When Knab did not reply, the Yareg chieftain hissed, "Well, it's us undone! We were readying boats to come to your succour; everyone knows of the enmity between Krannogberg and Sangspit! We had one longboat in the Bight when the blasts changed. We didn't have the time to get it back to shore and make a good defence when Sokaroth, that Sk'van-bedamned monster fell on us.

"We've lost fifteen men and all three of our longboats! All while you cowered behind that embankment of yours, built by all that silver you showered around the Bight!

"They might've taken more than just the boats if they hadn't caught sight of Ylfing sails coming down out of Dople. At least there's some what might come to our aid in the future."

The Narhaveners whose kin could pay *lifgyld*, nine of them, returned before the autumn, having passed a growing season labouring in Jarlag fields or a fishing season hauling on Jarlag nets. The other six were given over to the Sea Wolves as the Jarlag toll that year, preserving the community's reserves of grain, fish and meat. Only three of those six ever returned to Narhaven, and that was only years later after they had paid *lifgyld* again, for they had all already served the Sea Wolves for years, amassing their life price the first time around.

When Knab thought back on the raid on Narhaven, he knew that Sokaroth, far from sparing the Darnok, had dealt them an unexpected and costly blow. The Yareg and all the other folk on the Bight now believed that if the Jarlags returned, they could not hope for relief from Krannogberg. Knab, Kyre, and others spent much of the year trying to repair the relations with his neighbours, but the damage had been done. Though the Yareg took some barrels of fish and three bushels of barley readily enough, suspicion had crept into their eyes. Once again, both sides knew who had come out on top.

§

The strife with the Jarlags, and the regular visits, both hostile and otherwise, of the Sea Wolves puzzled Lora. When she was eight, she took her questions to the Darnok's priest, Magon Sokirth, a man who had dedicated his life to Hondrig, the Judge, the God who weighed the deeds of every soul, measuring them against the *wyrd* that the Dealer of Fates, Rulla, had given to each Fjordlander. Magon was old, nearing sixty, but he was yet hale and Lora found him that bright summer morning re-shingling the roof of his cottage. When she asked to speak with him, he scrambled down his ladder like a younger man and she felt his strength as he took her hand. "Come with me, young girl," he said, "and I shall answer your questions as best I may."

After receiving Loska's blessing, Magon guided Lora up the pathway that led to the plateau but took the branching half way up that led to a shelf in the hills that was protected from the north winds and that received more summer sun. The town's death cairns lay at one end of that long shelf, and at the other grew the trees of the Harrowood. The trees were mostly ancient oaks, but there were many spruce and the odd birch tree as well. Only Magon went there often, at least fortnightly, to pray. He also held the annual Brightnight festivities commemorating mid-summer, marriages and the celebrations of lives lived in that holy place. The folk believed that to go there without a solemn purpose or a priest was dangerous. To do so invited the attention of Heligat, Ruler of Skalagg, the Domain of the Dead, or, worse yet, Sk'van the Twisted, the Master of the Dark, a demon who captures the souls of the living. The Darnok only passed under its eaves if they were troubled or if they wanted to betroth themselves or make some other solemn proclamation before the Gods.

Magon led Lora down a groomed pathway to a dell in the middle of the woods. Shafts of sunlight streamed through the leaves, illuminating ferns and lily of the valley, thrushes darted among the tree trunks, and insects hummed in the daytime heat. The old priest bade her sit on one of several stumps that had been carved into smooth seats and that had been placed in a semi-circle facing the pathway down which they had walked. "Now, my lass, this is an appropriate place for inappropriate questions. There are no prying ears. What is it you would know and that you do not dare ask your mother?"

Lora looked into the priest's face, a face that had marked the passage of time but that ironically radiated both wisdom and youthful energy. "My, my ..." Lora stammered. She took a deep breath and blurted out, "My parents were Sea Wolves."

"Yes," Magon replied, waiting for more.

"You knew?"

"Yes, of course I knew. What is the matter, Lora?"

"Well, everyone's afraid of them coming to raid us! The last time they came, mother made me run for the cave with the other children. When we came back they had taken Erig and Lief. They take our grain and meat. Some have escaped them and settled here and they talk about how much they hated the Sea Wolves. If others knew that my parents were Sea Wolves, well ..."

Magon smiled and laid a hand on Lora's shoulder. "Ah, lass, I understand now. Yes, the Sea Wolves make us wary, but have you not noticed the anticipation among the young lads before they come? We give them our older boys so that the Sea Wolves can turn them into men. Surely you remember more than just Erig and Lief leaving ... what about young Henrik leaving with them two years ago?"

Lora nodded, though in truth she had forgotten Henrik.

"They wanted to go! They wanted to begin their passage to manhood.

"Listen, the Sea Wolves are a clan apart and so, yes, like other clans, they might raid us. But you need to understand that they are also unlike any other clan. They are a clan of warriors who protect us from other peoples who wish us ill.

All clans must give them what they need to survive, so yes, they come for a tithe of grain, fish and meat. And I should not forget ale and mead. They have always had a thirst on them."

Magon carried on, "We give them these things so that they can keep at sea and protect us. In the winter they sail to southern lands, to the lands of those who would kill or enslave us if they could. The Sea Wolves teach these people to fear and avoid us. Yes, they raid, as other clans raid us every now and then, or as sometimes we raid. But they do it for the most part in lands where there are riches for the taking. As you know, each man has a *lifgyld*, a life price, measured to a man's worth. Every man must serve the Sea Wolves until he has amassed enough to pay his *lifgyld*. Then he can start his new life as a freedman where he wants to step ashore. That's why people who settle here are happy to have left the Sea Wolves. They can live their lives as they see fit … within the bounds of the law, of course.

"This tradition keeps the various packs of Sea Wolves strong, with good boats and good weapons. It keeps the clans safe from our enemies, and eventually brings wealth and safety to our people. Think on Knab, when he came to Krannogberg, he had enough wealth to pay his *lifgyld* to the Sea Wolves, give *weregyld* to Yellik and build new houses, a ship, the wall around our village. He also brought others to live among us who brought their silver and their axes with them. Therefore, we are better and stronger because of the Sea Wolves."

Lora absorbed all this, thought about it and then asked, "But the Sea Wolves also attack our village. If they protect us, why do they attack us?"

"Well, men from many clans form each Sea Wolf clan. Some are composed of many of our enemies, particularly the Jarlags. These clans oft prefer the richer takings of a raid rather than the modest tithe that is more common for us these days. Indeed, little one, there are many Sea Wolves who have a taste for pleasures that we would not give them willingly, so when they come we send you away with our elders and the other children.

"But the day will come, my lass, when the Sea Wolves will come and part of their tithe will be your young friends. Just as you must spend a year with Torga Danail learning herb lore, the husbanding of animals - particularly their birthing - braving the wild animals that live near the mountains and practicing how to wield a spear ... you have started to learn the spear, no?"

Lora nodded dutifully.

"Well, good," Magon declared. "Just remember that until your own season of passing into adulthood, it's for fending off badgers, not Sea Wolves. That's a good way to die young. What I am saying to you, lass, is that those boys will leave one day and, if they return to Krannogberg, they will return as men. I deem you must ready yourself for that day."

Lora brooded on that for a long while.

§

As for Sea Wolves, rather than simply levying an annual tithe, an actual attack occurred only once. It was a night raid made by the Grey Wolves during a winter storm in the children's ninth year. Low-lying mist and driving snow hid the attack from both the watchtower and the redoubt. Another two of Knab's measures protected them that night; a watchman doing the rounds, Rolf at his heels, and the embankment-turned-wall. The night watchman - old Robin Sorik that night - took note of a sudden growl from Rolf, saw the dog's hackles rise as the cur sniffed the night air, and then beheld the Sea Wolf hulls emerging from the blowing snow. Rolf bayed to the Godspace and Sorik clanged his bell. The subsequent storming of the beach by the attackers stalled when they came to the well-defended stone-encased embankment that had finally fully enclosed Krannogberg the autumn before. The clash of arms claimed the life of one Grey Wolf, maimed a Krannogberger and led to a stand-off at the wall that was only resolved when four casks of Darnok salt meat were handed over to the Grey Wolves in exchange for their quiet departure.

Otherwise Knab's system worked well. If the various Sea Wolf clans approached with their chieftain's shield hung on the mast, then one fire arrow shot far before them served to honour their arrival. If no shield hung on the mast, the archer in the redoubt rained fire arrows directly down upon the attackers. In the eighth year of Knab's chieftainship - a year of poor harvests and empty fishing nets - some of the Sea Wolf clans grew hungry and remembered the building wealth of the Darnok. Twice the chieftains only hung their shields from their masts after their crews had to put out several on-board fires. Krannogberg slowly developed a reputation for not being worth the risk of a careless attack.

In those years, the greatest danger to the four children came from their own mishaps and rashness. When they were nine, Leigh and Fallig took all four bairns up to the summer ranges, not just their own son Cairn. So it was that Lora, Lars, and Thay, instead of fishing or crabbing, learnt the skills necessary for life at the foot of the Boldring Mountains. It was a time of joy for the four of them, passing their first summer together, but some of that joy was mixed with tears. Each one of them could already sit atop a horse, but Fallig put them through proper training. She had them stand on the horses' backs, hang over their necks, swing a stick from the saddle, all to familiarize the children with the anatomy of the horse and develop skill in positioning oneself in relation to the horse's body. She had them practice pivoting their mounts, do running leaps to mount them and dismount from a trotting horse - Lora even mastered doing so by somersaulting. Then Fallig had the children gallop, rear their horses, leap over obstacles. At this point, Thay, who had hitherto spent more time in fishing boats with his father than around animals, took a spill and broke an arm. In the end, he did more brooding than riding that summer and could only look on as the others practiced shooting an arrow from a galloping pony.

During the following winter, at Lora's prompting, they stole some sparring shields - that had no shield bosses - and climbed the fjord where the snows lay thick upon the ground. They found a place they liked with a long slope giving way to a flat that overlooked a precipice that plunged down to the Harrowood. They took turns running, leaping through the air, landing on the shields, and scooting down the slope, coming to a halt on the flat. Lora, first at everything, shot down the hill in a fit of laughter. Lars and Thay followed, likewise shrieking their joy into the cold air. However, when Cairn's turn came, he slid down the slope hollering with glee, until he realized that his greater momentum was carrying him further across the flat than the others. He spun off the shield, trying to slow down in the snow, but he rolled past his horrified friends and slid over the lip of the cliff. He fell barely the height of a man into the branches of the only stunted tree that clung to the cliff. Old Magon adjudged that either Guliveg, who tends the spark of life, or Florri, who bestows good fortune, must have protected Cairn from disaster, though neither protected the young lad from Fallig, his mother; he spent the rest of the winter labouring on the crafting of snowshoes with Old Wobbly rather than tramping around outside with his friends.

When the bairns turned eleven, their parents brought them together in the home of Loska and Uilig, Lora's parents, for a birthday celebration. The children soon realized it was a more serious affair than those of other years. First, Thülla, Thay's mother, stood before them, looming thin and tall, taller than anyone present except Leigh, Cairn's father. Her honey-yellow hair flowed around her stern face and fell to the small of her back. She gave them a penetrating look with her grey eyes ... the look that always stopped Thay in mid-mischief. "This birthday is not like those that came before. You are now ready to learn the skills of adulthood. From this day henceforth, you must contribute to the Darnok's labours. You shall mend nets, tend flocks, and make flax and berries flourish so that we have sustenance to survive our winters. You shall lay stone, cut turf, and plane wood so that we have shelter to protect us from the Tears of the Ghosts. You shall ripple flax for linen, spin wool, and weave leg-wraps and sew together sails so that we can survive our nights under the Godspace and sail the seas. You shall pluck feathers, plane shafts, and carve yew so that we can take down the wild goose or the raider from a distance with a bow and arrow. You shall sharpen iron, heft a round shield, swing an axe, and wield a blade so that we can defend ourselves from our enemies."

Of course the children cheered upon hearing the last phrase, and Thülla did her best to remain serious. She took an axe from her husband, Rig, and held it out to Thay. "This is your grandfather's axe, *Tear Tongue*. It tasted Jarlag blood within a year of the Darnok leave-taking from the Darnalths of Jorrumsfjord after we first brought steadings to the Andersfjord. May the strength of its iron keep you alive until the call of its history brings you back to Krannogberg some day." She cracked one of her rare smiles at that and added, "Though if I have to choose between you making your home elsewhere and receiving that axe back from your friends, I'll let you go live in Tok's Harbour in the far north if need be." The young, tawny-haired lad took the axe and felt its full weight. He looked at its dull iron head, its polished wood, its thong that allowed it to be hung from the wrist. The haft had runes carved into its wood; he recognized a couple, the rune for Tanat ... according to local legend, his maternal grandfather was always one to play the fool ... and the rune for daring. Although awed by the moment, disappointment gnawed at him. The runes felt right, the weapon somehow did not.

Rena disturbed his thinking as she stepped forward and handed Lars a similar weapon. "You will have to give this one a name, for its only feat of renown was to open a hole in the ice of the Tallogswater one winter, allowing my father and I to fish when we were hungry as all Skalagg! Its make is sound, though, and it can prevent you from dying as well as one with a name."

Lars didn't seem bothered that the axe had no name. His eyes lit up as his thoughts ran ahead of him. "Well then, let's use one of Kyre's kennings to name it! You used it to get fish, you say? What about *Fjordbird*?"

Rena nodded and declared, "What about it indeed!"

Fallig then stood and handed a short-handled axe to Cairn. "This is a short weapon, even for a young lad like yourself." She saw in her son's eyes that her words had sparked a flash of disappointment so she held up a finger to keep him silent a moment longer. "It's a fine weapon, my boy, crafted for speed and use in close quarters. Something tells me you'll be more one for bear hugs than a yew bow! And sure, you'll have your maul."

Cairn looked up. "What maul?"

Fallig smiled and turned to Leigh, who hefted to her a heavy sack. "Cairn Soleigh, I give you," she opened the sack, pulled out a thick length of polished oak, "*Orgor's Awl*. The Great Crafter uses His awl to punch holes in shield walls."

"Though unlike an awl, you have to hold it the other way around," piped in Leigh.

"I sussed that out, father," Cairn replied with a chuckle. He took the heavy weapon from his mother, holding it more gently than he would a baby. Its handle was yet big for his hands, but it had spiralling wooden ridges and a knob at its butt to prevent it from flying out of one's grip in battle.

It stood nearly as tall as its eleven year-old wielder and became thicker as it rose to its head. Along its length it sported the runes for Orgor and Karn, the Goddess of War, carved into its length and painted red on the shining golden wood. "Sure, it's a fine, fine thing, and solid, though I don't doubt Lars' head would put a dent in it!"

Lars shoved his stout friend and shouted "Ach! Vermin! Mind your words or *Fjordbird* will bite your bum!" Cairn crashed his shoulder against Lars in retaliation, sending the blonde boy staggering backwards, but they all had a good laugh.

Finally Loska, an impressive woman built for a fight and who had sailed with the Sea Wolves in her youth, held out a scabbard to Lora. "As a girl, you will be expected to hunt on the plateau with a spear to become a woman, and you will certainly learn the use of an axe, but I would have you learn how to wield this as well." Lora took the scabbard and withdrew a beautiful seax. The tip of its polished oak handle featured the head of an ice bear done in rare steel, with a ring of the same metal dangling from behind the teeth of its muzzle. A loop and two bolts, these made from brass, bound the long blade to the handle. The blade itself was steel, and it was well cared-for, also polished so that no stain or spot of rust could be found. For its first six thumb-lengths it had a similar shape to a large knife, though it had a long runnel along its top, but for its last half-dozen thumb-lengths, it arced at first downwards before its point crept upwards ever so slightly. Where the runnel ended, about five thumb-lengths along the top of the blade, runic markings carried on. Its blade featured a wavy pattern, like the snakes of blowing snow driven before the blizzard.

Lora gaped at its beauty, though the boys, too, looked upon it with awe. "It is called *Íss*, for the ice of our land, and your grandmother first used it. She gave it to me when I left Jorrumsfjord with the Sea Wolves, only shortly before the Jarlags sacked it." Loska said. "It is too big for you now, but may it long defend you during your journey through this world."

For the rest of that winter, they began weapons training during the long nights in the village roundhouse.

Early in the spring of that same year, Fallig spotted a real, living ice bear on the plateau. A party of warriors went up to kill it or chase it off so that there would be no danger when the herds were taken up to the hills. Given their newfound skill handling horses, Lora, Lars, and Cairn joined the party to take care of the short, shaggy mounts should the warriors need to dismount, leaving a despondent, silent Thay behind. Lo, the band of warriors tracked the beast to a wood, rumoured to be haunted, on the plateau. They dismounted and entered the forest on foot, leaving the youngsters with the horses. Lora and Lars helped Cairn tether the mounts, tying their reins about the boughs of trees with slip knots. Then they amused themselves by moving down the meadow a ways to spar with their spears without bothering the horses. Cairn amused himself by pulling his cloak tightly about his frame and stretching out with his back against a tree. Soon the clack of spear shaft on spear shaft became hard to hear over Cairn's snoring.

The day dragged on until suddenly the white bear burst from the trees downwind of them. It hefted its massive head, sniffed the wind, and turned towards them, pawing at the earth and slavering. And then it roared and charged, loping towards them with startling speed. The horses neighed in panic and strained at their tethers until the three youngsters tugged at their bonds, slipping the knots and letting them gallop away. Lora pulled Lars towards the woods, yelling for Cairn to join them. They retreated before the bear as it swerved after the scattering herd. It chased after the horses in vain for a dozen paces or so before coming to a halt. It watched the horses disappear over a nearby rise, and then it pivoted its bulk, lowered its head and roared once more. The youths backed into the forest as the ice bear dashed in its lumbering, yet rapid, gait towards them again. They kept together as best they could, putting the largest of the stunted trees between themselves and the bear, spears keeping the predator at bay, shields ready for the expected attack. Their hearts raced and their nostrils filled with the musky stink of the animal. They yelled and yelled, calling for help and hoping to scare the huge beast. A seeming eternity passed, filled with mock charges, half-hearted probing attacks from the bear, with heavy paws and claws sweeping at their spears, before it gave one full-on charge, roaring to the Godspace. They dodged around a large tree, scrambling backwards over roots and between brambles, their spears levelled at the beast. Lora and Lars stuck it, and though they did not wound it badly, they forced it to retreat. Help finally came. Knab led the attack that drove the bear off for good, but all the Darnok knew again that either Guliveg or Florri had been with the children that day.

Chapter Four

After turning twelve, the children had developed enough skill at adults' tasks to work without supervision. Cairn tended to the herds that summer and became a truly able rider. Leigh also taught him to smelt small amounts of iron from bog ore harvested from the surrounding heath. Lora had quick fingers, so she was put to fletching, and she learnt how to pull a bow and place the arrows she had made in the centre of a target more times than not up to thirty paces. She proved a capable hunter, able to take down an eider duck or rabbit that would go into the evening stew. Lars and Thay - and sometimes Lora - had to work on the fishing boats, not simply as helpers who could hand around midday trenchers or whose nimble fingers could defeat a tricky knot in a fishing line. Adjusting to the new reality came harder for Thay; the days were gone when he could lie back, gaze at the clouds and dream of leading the Darnok warriors against the Jarlags. He had to leave behind the etherial claymore of his reverie, or even more practical pastimes like picking up Straelish words from Aganas with Lora, and instead haul ropes and set nets.

The sodden weight of the nets slowly added muscle to Thay's previously lanky frame while their biting frigidity built his character, proving to him over time that he could endure hardship and need not shy from it. He hated the labour but, being quiet by nature, he didn't complain about the blisters or the numb hands - unlike Lars, who often could be heard across the water griping from a neighbouring boat. Indeed, Thay loved the time with his father. Of those days he remembered song, sea, and stories more than the endless work. In the grey light of dawn every day they rowed out from shore, down the fjord, past the watch tower, and out into the Bight. They heaved the nets over the gunnels, set the wooden floats and rowed further out. Thay's muscles throbbed and pulsed by midday. When the time came to pull in the nets in the evening, his arms and shoulders felt dead. He became a more patient, quieter lad as he pondered his father's fate, a man who had accepted leaving a life with the Sea Wolves to become a fisher. Though he did not complain, he resolved to become more than a fisher and he used the time on the boat to hone his determination to rise to greatness, perhaps even to that golden torc that Kyre oft sang was promised to the Darnok by Helgya's visions.

Although some of his friends would still revel at the end of a long day in the songs and stories of Kyre the Bard - Lars sometimes lending his voice to the songs or providing accompaniment on a bone flute the bard had made for him - Thay could not muster the energy to join them. When Thay's father Rig had tied up the boat for the night, the youngster would fall into his bed and lose himself instantly in sleep. The dreams of the winged worm disturbed him not a bit when he first started on the water. Just prior to Brightnight, or mid-summer night, his father asked him about his dreams while rowing out to retrieve a net. "So, lad," he said, "you're growing so much these days I'm feared you'll turn into a bear, never mind a man." He paused for a moment in mid-stroke and asked, "Is it always the worms, lad? Do you never dream of bears, like what attacked the others last year?"

Thay shook his tawny-haired head and sighed, a look of uncharacteristic timidity crossing his freckled, fair face. After a while he replied, "I dunno Dad. It's neither at present. I'm too weary to dream. Sure, I've always had other dreams. All sorts of things happen in them and the creatures of the hills and forests speak to me at times. But when a crimson dream comes, aye ..."

Rig waited, and waited some more, but finally prompted his son, " 'When a crimson dream comes' ...?"

Thay shrugged. " 'tis always the winged worm what speaks to me."

"*Crimson dreams.* You've never called them nightmares. The worm doesn't scare you?"

Thay's grey eyes lost their focus as he gazed across the water, hardly taking in the shapes of Lora and her father Uilig pulling in their lobster traps never mind the fjords and the mountains in the distance. At length he sighed and said, "I dunno." This time Rig waited, remembering what it was like to be a twelve-year-old boy. Thay found his voice again, and it had lost its youthful timidity, "I honestly don't understand it, father. It is hard for me to put into words. She's never filled me with dread, only awe. Some dreams do terrify me, some don't. It's as if she shows me some things happening in far away places. Some are horrible things, some are not. Often the dreams are ... well ... like normal daydreams; I get the feeling that they're simply a love of flight and desire for rest. I'm sorry, father. It vexes me that I can't put it any better than that."

Rig nodded and then rowed against the drift that had swept them away from their lines. After a while he stated, "I can't pretend to know what it all means, Thay, but only a fool would dismiss it as worthless. There's something in your future, lad. I just hope that it's benign."

Thay nodded and reached a long arm for the next line.

§

As Brightnight neared, Thay and his father stayed out on the water more and more. While the sun would creep towards the grey line where sea met sky, it refused to disappear completely and even Rig could not work without respite. Once the watchtower on shore became obscured in the twilight of the middle night, he would end the day's work, to the obvious relief of Thay. He would take the oars and let his son lie on the nets at the prow of the small boat. He would smile to himself, and to the persistent sun, when he invariably heard Thay's soft snoring.

Although he toiled without complaint, Thay prayed to Norrgi and tried any number of cantrips before falling into bed in the often forlorn hope that a fierce summer wind would rise. On those very rare days that Norrgi deigned to respond favourably to Thay's entreaties and blow in a storm, the youngster slept and mended nets more than he played games of heroism and conquest with Lars and Lora, a change from his younger years. Lars and Lora, too, played such games less, with the lanky blonde lad learning the basics of the harp from Kyre or deepening his skill with his bone flute, and the energetic girl fletching, hunting or learning the secrets of brewing beer from her mother. On those days that Thay could sneak off with his friends, they all found their amusement incomplete in the absence of Cairn.

One blustery day after middle summer while Thay scrubbed at a blackened pot, out from the low-hanging mist that flew before the blasting wind, Lars came running up to the cottage. He stopped in front of Thay, panting, but his long face beamed with excitement, his ice blue eyes sparkled and his striking blonde shoulder-length hair flapped in the wind. "Thay," he gasped, "Come! Come quickly!"

"What? Why? What's got you wailing like a rutting elk?"

Lars cast a furtive look about and then stretched up on his toes to look over Thay's shoulder through the threshold of the cottage to make sure Thay's mother, Thülla, wasn't around to overhear. He leaned forward and whispered, "I found a claymore up in the meadow."

Thay's eyes widened. "Whose is it, do you know?"

"No, I don't. Come on!" Thay threw on a cloak to protect him from the blowing drizzle and then the two of them went in search of Lora. The visibility was poor with the mist and the occasional squall of blowing rain, but they knew their way without the aid of their eyes. They found her sweeping out her family's brew shed after having made a mess adding barley to her latest batch of beer. When Lars told her of the find, her eyes went wide in astonishment. Despite her obvious excitement, she drove the boys to distraction by calmly putting away her broom, hanging up her apron, turning to the barrel and giving the brew one last stir. When the lads' protested their impatience, she held up a finger and replied, "My mother says that swords take lives whereas beer sustains them." She donned her coat, turned to Lars and ordered, "Now, take us to see this thing."

The calm could last no longer and the three bolted off through the mist as quickly as their feet could carry them. Thay marvelled at Lars' and Lora's speed; it never occurred to him that his own body bore greater bulk after having worked all summer in the boat with his father. When finally they reached the middle vale, gasping for breath and bursting with excitement, Lars led his friends in the opposite direction to the Harrowood, leading them to the old chestnut tree that stood alone on the heath, halfway between the Harrowood and the Darnok's burial cairns. Its uppermost boughs were lost in the sheets of mist and drizzle blasting past. There stood the claymore, all dull and menacing with its tip stuck into the ground. "I found it over there," Lars gushed, pointing to a nearby overhang in the fjord wall. "It was all covered in dirt and grime." Lora wrinkled her nose at that. Lars felt he had to add, "I wasn't wallowing in it! I was looking for mushrooms! I stuck it here before going to get you."

Lars took the sword from the ground and showed it to his friends. It had all the traits of the great swords that chieftains coveted as symbols of their status: the long blade with fullers on each face, though these were filled with encrusted dirt; the long hand guards sloping out and away from the pommel; the knobbed ends of those guards worked into the likeness of cords tied into knots; the pommel itself worked with what appeared to be silver wire for the grip; and, finally, the rounded knob of the butt inlaid with a green gem. Also worked into the pommel were nine gleaming stones forming the constellation loved by Hondrig, the Scales; one gemstone set above two others to either side, and each of those two had three gemstones arced under it.

Thay and Lora looked on wide-eyed as Lars grasped the hilt and hoisted the weapon. Lars gave it a couple of hearty swings before levelling its rusty point at Thay's chest. "Well I'll be a beached whale!" Thay gasped. Lars stabbed it into the ground again and the sound it made when its tip hit a stone made Lora grimace.

"Don't treat it like that, Lars," she chided. "It deserves better! Give it over." She held out her hand.

"Ach, Lora, it's stronger than any stone," Lars replied, though he offered her the pommel. "And sure, I don't mind cleaning it up and sharpening it. It will be my very own claymore that I'll take into battle."

Lora gave it a couple of sweeps, lopping off the bulbous, flowering heads of nearby nettles. "Ay! It's heavy, is it not? Too heavy for me at any rate."

"It's made for a man's strength," Lars declared with a deliberate nod, his blonde hair spilling over his blue eyes.

"Well then, you'll not soon be using it in battle either, will you?" she retorted.

Taking the sword back from Lora, Lars asked, "What should I name it?"

"*Harbinger,*" Thay responded without a moment's thought. The other two gave him puzzled looks. "Sure, that's what it is; a harbinger."

"A harbinger of what?" Lora asked. Thay noticed her look had changed, from awed to thoughtful, curious.

"Greatness, what else?" he replied.

"Greatness?" Lars queried. "How can you be so sure? You're no seer."

"Of course it'll bring greatness, you ass." Thay retorted. "It's got the markings of the Scales, in homage to Hondrig. And sure, our clan will become the largest, richest and most powerful clan among the fjords. This is just another sign."

Lora laughed before asking, "And I suppose Thay the Wise has seen other such signs?"

"Yes there've been others. We've seen naught of the Sea Wolves for ages, the ice bears haven't touched our sheep this year, and remember the song Kyre sings of what that old seeress, Helgya Darik once said; our clan will foster a child that will forge new customs and wear the golden torc of a king about his throat." Then he added with a smile, "It might be Lars here, though he's too pretty to bloody himself! Most like 'tis me!"

"Ha!" shouted Lars. "You mongrel! For that, I'll skewer you with *Harbinger*!"

He grasped the hilt and pursued Thay around the meadow, the two of them laughing so loud that Rig heard them as he walked down from the high pastures, where despite the drizzle and wind he had gone hunting rabbit for the evening supper. Thay's father was astonished to see the spectacle and quickly intervened, pulling the claymore from a horrified Lars and grasping Thay's ear. "What are the three of you doing here?" he demanded. Before any of the children could respond, he turned to Thay and snarled, "You are supposed to be mending nets, young lad, and where did you steal this?"

"Lars found it!" Thay cried. "We didn't steal it!" Lars nodded, trembling in terror.

"Aye, well, we'll soon see to the truth of that," he declared. Holding Thay by the collar of his cloak with one hand, and clutching brace of rabbits with the other, he marched the youngsters down to the village and straight into the roundhouse. "You sit there," he ordered, forcing Thay onto a stool before the great dais. Then he pointed to other stools clear on the other side of the fire pit. "Lars, Lora, sit there. None of you are to say a word until ordered to do so. Understand?"

"Y ... yes, sir," Thay stammered. Rig gave him a wallop. "I didn't order you to speak. A simple nod will do." Thay cowered on the stool while Lars and Lora scampered across to the others. Rig placed the claymore at the foot of the chieftain's chair and left the roundhouse. Not long after, villagers arrived and cast disparaging looks at the three youngsters before drawing stools and sitting around the dais. Slowly the hall filled and with every new soul that entered, Thay felt his heart sink deeper and deeper into his guts.

He had long since given up thoughts of escape and resigned himself to punishment - though he hoped Knab would take pity upon him - when his sister Ellena arrived. Rather than make nasty faces at him, she took no notice of her younger sibling at all. He gave up all hope of salvation when finally his mother arrived, tall and proud, but instead of crossing to him and scolding him for leaving the cottage without permission, she settled into a stool far to his left, crossed her hands upon her lap and stared at the chair on the dais in silence.

One by one the summertime population of the Darnok filled the roundhouse. The wind that howled between the cottages meant that all the fisher folk, like Thay himself, were about for the summoning, and so the place brimmed with people as though they were about to proclaim a war. Indeed, for some reason, many of the folk had come geared out for battle, wearing boiled leather or mail, and carrying weapons and shields. The place filled with noise, though, as people chatted and laughed. Thay felt his terror mount with the rising noise and bustle of the roundhouse until, as he thought he would burst apart in a spray of blackness, the chat halted. Instead of easing his concern, however, the sudden silence seized his heart with talons of ice.

Thay kept his eyes focussed on the chieftain's chair in front of him but he did not have to wait long to see who had entered the roundhouse. Magon Sokirth, the village's Priest of Hondrig, stood upon the dais in his full ceremonial robes and looked around the hall. Magon was now ancient and slowing down, though still in good health. His full, grey beard still flowed past his neck and onto his chest. He sat on the stool to the right of the chieftain's chair. Knab was the last to come in, escorted by Kyre. As Knab took his place, dressed normally as though he had nothing more to do that day than mend nets, he noted the arms and armour and asked the other Krannogbergers, "Planning a wee raid without me?" No one laughed. He nodded to Magon and the old priest began an invocation to Hondrig. When the holy rites were complete, Knab placed his hands on his knees and declared, "We are in moot ... though I still have no idea why." He nudged the claymore before his chair with his foot, "though perhaps it's to do with this. Would someone care to tell me?"

" 'Tis my will that we gather, my chieftain," Magon replied, "after listening to the words of Rig Sowulf."

"Explain yourself."

"I shall, my chieftain. I shall indeed. You see, these three young mischief makers found yon claymore on the heath."

Lars leapt to his feet, "I found the claymore."

Renith, Lars' father, stood and pushed the boy back onto the stool. "Quiet, boy."

"No father," Lars blurted out an urgent response. "Knab needs it told true. I found the sword. I brought Lora and Thay up to see it later."

Knab held out his hand to Renith, forestalling the man's backhand blow. "Hold! In this your lad has the right of things. If it's so important we need a moot, then I want it all exact."

Renith nodded and sat back down in a clatter of chain mail. Magon also nodded, this time to Lars, acknowledging the correction, and then he continued, "This morning, young Lars found yon claymore on the heath. Rig, in turn, found them and remembered words where perhaps others would have forgotten. You see, the find made him think of a verse of Helgya's he heard many years ago now. It warned of something, just we did not know what. Rig has a quick mind and thinks it might serve now as a warning for us."

"What verse was this?" Knab asked.

"Helgya, bless her soul, was delirious and remembered naught of it. It went like this:

> Such sights I see as make me quake,
> such woe for us as makes me weep:
> a foreign lord with foreign arms
> and sowing, here, foreign woes.
>
> Such sights I see as make me fear,
> such strife that rips us from our kin:
> a choppy sea assailing reefs
> and wrecking, there, Fjordland's folk.
>
> Such sights I see as make me warn,
> such swans of death that gorge on flesh:
> a sorry clan on Jarlag ships
> lest Darnok, quickly, gather here.
>
> Such sights I see that make me hope,
> such deeds so great they dull the grief:
> a sorrow-claw of rusting steel,
> forsaken, here, on Darnok heath.
>
> That sight is key to make me smile,
> such light to chase the dark away;
> three wielders fall from faithless steel,
> to crown one here, a king's acclaim.

Knab leaned forward, "So you think it a warning linked to this sword?" Magon shrugged.

"I do," Rig responded, standing up. To Thay, his father seemed to stand taller, prouder. He gleamed in his chain mail. He had picked up an impressive shield during his days with the Sea Wolves; a tall, steel rectangle curved back on the left and right sides. It was embossed with a stylized ball of fire, beaten out from the metal in relief, falling from the sky. Rig had painted the fireball orange on a pitch background. He had laid his helm on the floor beside him, had set his right hand to rest on the head of his battle axe that was looped to his belt, and his left steadied his great shield. Thay had never seen his father decked out in his fighting gear and he felt his throat constrict in pride, and in fear. Rig continued, "For many years I have worked that verse over and over in my head and wondered what in the hells it meant. Oft I thought Tanat the Rogue was toying with me. But I took one look at that sword and thought of the verse. Look at it, Knab. It's a noble blade, forged of steel, not iron. And yet rust has gotten at it. It made me think immediately of 'a sorrow-claw of rusting steel, forsaken, here, on Darnok heath.' I spoke my mind to Magon. He agreed." Magon nodded, a stern look upon his countenance.

"And you think this sword is some portent?"

"The verse warns us to gather here. The blade may be no more than a device for achieving that aim. But of course, as is the case with any prophesy, it may be much, much more than a simple device."

"But this will be the blade of our king!" Lars exclaimed, jumping again from his stool.

Knab turned his face to the young lad and warned, "Don't push your luck, stripling. You can remain quiet now." Lars, chastised, nodded and sat back down. Knab glanced over the boy's shoulder at Renith and demanded, "What is this gibberish your lad speaks about a king?" The hall fell into silence at the chief's slight at the village's lore.

Renith, also clad for battle and in no mood to play it meek, held the chieftain's gaze and replied, "They were the visions of our old seeress. Helgya Darik was our last soothsayer; she had a vision and spoke of a king, or *kunungr*, a day before the Sea Wolves let you come ashore."

If Knab took any offence at the stab at his subjected status among the Sea Wolves, he did not let it show. He simply nodded - perhaps thinking the prophesy might touch his own fate - and asked, "Not all seeresses always see true. Did she?"

Magon stepped forward, paused and looked about at the faces of the villagers. He stated in a voice that brooked no debate, "Her words have worked themselves into the soul of the clan. As near as I can tell, she saw true more often than not, and the times she didn't, I'd put the blame on the interpreter, not her. Her words that day, well, I'd place more stock in them if they weren't her last visions, told when fevered and on her deathbed. Even so, I would not gainsay her."

"What was this last vision?"

Magon glowered about the roundhouse before turning to the chieftain again. "You might have heard it from foolish children like these three before us, or from our bard, Kyre, who has set much of our Darnok lore to verse.

"After Helgya died that night, you see, I committed her verse to memory so that I could talk to Hondsar about it the next day. I never had the opportunity, for you came, my chieftain. I have never spoken it to anyone until now, though Hondrig knows that Kyre pressed me hard enough to confirm what the women told him. His version is a close approximation and already many here will recognize its strains, but I do not think he has had it true, until today, of course. He'll have it in his mind now. Helgya's vision went like this:

From Andersfjord on Hondrig's Bight,
one shall rise to highest heights,
reforge our world, recast our dreams:

Florri's wayward child,
Orgor's chosen one,
Rulla's greatest rune.

From foreign lands to Fjordland's shores,
one shall come to challenge lore,
reshape our folk, cast off our chains:
Asgear's favoured hand,
Karn's blessed warrior
Tanat's sorrow-claw.

To unknown ends and waters new,
one shall guide our longboat crews,
reward the brave, reweigh His scales:
Norrgi's sou'west wind,
Rulla's fylgja owl,
Darnok's kunungr-torc.

"I don't ken the half of it." Magon sighed deeply. "I don't ken the fifth of it. Sure, there is at least one kenning therein I recognize and some strange words. As Rig says, a 'sorrow-claw' is often a sword. Perhaps young Lars is right, it may be the same one from the verse that prompted the summons to gather here. I note that the sorrow-claw occurs at the end of the second vísa or grouping of words in the chant. Does that mean 'kunungr's torc' represents something else or is it supposed to be taken at face value? It doesn't follow the usual accepted form of a kenning.

"As for some words we don't use often, I believe most of us know the tale of the *fylgja*, an animal embodying the spirit of a master. Our great Goddess, Rulla, has one. She is the Mistress of Owls and owls are a type of *fylgja* for wisdom. And what of *kunungr*, what those beyond the Teeth call a king?

"One meaning of this song might be that our fjord will foster a child who will cause to pass here in Fjordland a transformation in rule of the kind seen abroad and in so doing perhaps place a golden torc of a *kunungr* about his throat. I know not what to think of it, but it seems this might be a transformation imposed at the end of a sorrow-claw! Is that what we really want?"

Thay stared into the fire at the centre of the roundhouse and shivered.

That was when Rolf, old, old Rolf the Steadfast, barked.

Chapter Five

Rolf hardly barked any more. He was old, having passed his fifteenth birthing day. His back legs seemed to have a mind of their own and he had trouble getting to his feet. His hearing was no good any more and he never joined his voice to the peal of the watchman's bell whenever it rang, unless he actually saw someone swinging it. The days were long gone when he joined in the periodic fights for dominance among the village curs; he had never achieved the chieftainship but he was the best loved dog and the others seemed to know it. In his fighting days, whenever he had gotten involved in a losing squabble, there was always someone who had come running to kick the fighters apart and make sure Rolf was unhurt. He had always had the knack of being just a little hurt, needing the village healer's attention and a bowl of broth to put things right. Afterwards, when his muzzle had turned more grey than black, the young, dominant dogs gave him his space as though he were a breed apart, occupying a place between the common hounds and the people who strode like gods upon their earth. They saw those gods stopping in midstride to kneel down to the old one, the one who slept so much during the day, but who patrolled the strand with the watchmen every night without fail.

That blustery, sodden day with mist blowing off the Andersfjord and through the town, the watchmen might have been called to the moot, but Rolf was not one to set aside his duties so easily. Perhaps noticing that something was amiss, that everyone was in the roundhouse and that there was none of the normal activity of the town going on, Rolf had roused himself from his slumber on the doorstep of Kyre's cottage. He had limped about the village, sniffing at the usual sites, making sure all was in order, over-marking where necessary, before making his way down to the strand. Although he could hardly see now, he peered into the mist of the fjord regardless. His useless ears perked up, but more in reaction to something on the wind than any sound that came to him. He raised his nose and sniffed again, his hackles rising. An echo of a memory came to him, carried on that wind, and he trotted down the beach to the water, moving faster than he had in a year. Again he raised his nose to the wind, moving his head left and then right.

Barking like mad took a lot of energy, but the scent of intruders was a stimulant like no other. Rolf heaved in a deep breath and let loose like a dog in his prime, like the dog he was when the Jarlags attacked Krannogberg after Knab became chieftain.

A hush fell over the roundhouse. It lasted only a moment before the town's other dogs raised their voices, spurring Rig to action. He jumped to his feet in his battle regalia and called to Knab, "I'll anchor the defence 'til you get there." Knab nodded and the village flew into action.

"Get your gear!" Knab yelled, unnecessarily, before grabbing Loska, Lora's mother, and asking, "You know what to do?" She nodded. "Good. Do it." He leapt from the dais and bounded for his cottage. Nearly two score of the younger women armed themselves; they were shield wenches and while they might not join a shield wall, they could protect one's flanks or defend the town's curtain wall. Loska ordered the actions of the older women, getting them to round up the youngsters and setting them on the path to the redoubt. She turned to the three youngsters. "And what of you three?" she asked.

Of course Lora replied, "We can run quickly if need be, Mum, but until then, we can put out fires or drag the wounded back from the fight. I can put a few arrows in them!"

"Or stick *Harbinger* in anyone who comes at us from our backs," Lars blurted.

"No!" Loska snapped. "You'll do no such thing! Not just yet. Get buckets of water and hoes. Keep your eyes out for fires and deal with them. If we start failing, do not waste a moment. Run! Run like the very *tosk-hyr* of the forest were at your heels, do you understand me?" They nodded. "Good. Go get the hoes and water!" They darted off. She bit her lip, heaved a sigh, then called after Lora. "Daughter!" Lora spun around. "Do you ... do you see yourself putting arrows in them?" Lora's flecked blue eyes flashed, she licked her lips, but then she nodded. Loska waved a hand towards their family cottage, "Get your bow and a quiver of arrows, then get your hoe." She watched her daughter dart off to her home, then she donned her armour.

The embankment that the Darnok had raised when Knab became chieftain had imposed a shape on Krannogberg: square. Over the intervening years, the spaces that the embankment had enclosed had filled with the odd cottage, a smithy and racks for drying fish. Also over those years, progressive work of the townsfolk had transformed the embankment into a proper stone wall. It was now about two feet thick and rose to shoulder height of a tall man like Knab. Merlons rose from its crest, protecting defenders who could stab with longspears through the crenels down at attackers who themselves would have to scramble across the ditch encircling the wall. The wall only sported two entrances: a small iron gate firmly anchored into the east wall, behind the village, that gave on to the paths that led up to the plateau; and, an eight-foot wide open archway at the front of the village, facing west, that gave onto the shingle beach. The archway was the only feature that broke the square shape of the wall, for it was set back a halfdozen feet and on either side the wall bent inwards to meet the beginning of the archway.

Rig, Renith, Old Wobbly, Uilig, and Roben formed an initial shield wall in that open gap under the arch in the town's curtain wall. They did so none too soon for the shapes of longboats emerged from the mist and drizzle. Seven of them scraped up onto the gravel beach and waves of warriors hopped over the sides. "Seven," Renith muttered as he anchored his shield into a groove in the stones under the arch.

"Seven," Old Wobbly confirmed, smiling and setting his own shield into the groove. "Upwards of five hundred men. But they don't know Krannogberg, do they?"

He smiled because Knab knew something of raiding and had a cunning mind. The chieftain had built up the town's defences so that raiders would fall into carefully designed traps, such as a wall with an undefended archway eight feet wide. What attacker wouldn't make for the gap? Knab had set it back from the perimeter with those angled walls so that attackers would get funnelled together, compressing themselves and restricting their own movement. He had paved the space inside the walls with large flagstones to give defenders better footing than the shingle outside the arch that would give way under attackers' feet. He had also set that groove into the stones under the archway so that defenders could set their lower shield edge in it and make a shield wall more resistant to pressure. A solid shield anchored in place would give a defender confidence and allow him to pay more attention to stabbing through the gaps in the shield wall rather than worrying about his safety.

Although they looked it, the stones atop the archway were not fixed with mortar. Instead, they were set upon a wooden cradle that could be tipped forward with the pull on a chain from inside the wall, tipping a ton of rock directly in front of the archway. Murder holes had been designed into the funnelling stonework of the angled walls, allowing defenders to stab spears into the flanks of any attackers surging towards the gap in the wall or trying to flee. Weighted nets, reserves of caltrops, and concealed pits set beyond the ditch around the embankment all formed part of Krannogberg's defences.

Knab had tinkered and tinkered with his ideas and plans over the years, but they hadn't been tested fully, until that day when the Jarlags and their Ilkaren and Jorgor allies decided to sack Krannogberg.

The attackers scrambled up the beach. The first defenders to meet them were the barking dogs, harrying but keeping their distance. They scattered in the face of the front assault, only to flash in from the flanks to rip at leg bindings, which, combined with the unstable footing of the shingle beach, spilled several men to the ground. Rigald Sokaroth led the first wave up the beach and he waved his men towards the archway. That first wave crashed against the reenforced shield wall ... and came to a thudding halt. They quickly found themselves stuck, pushed on by the press of more men Sokaroth waved forward, all eager for their numbers to overwhelm the seemingly feeble defence. The attackers threw themselves again against the defending shields. That was when Hild Dathagar pulled the chain, spilling the stones of the arch in front of the defensive shield wall and onto the attackers. The falling stone crushed the men in the first two ranks and threw a cluttered barrier in front of the attack. Spears stabbed from the wall at the men who tried to scramble around the pile of rubble and men.

A score of men had fallen - either crushed or speared - before Sokaroth pulled men away from the back of the press and sent them to attack the wall to the north and south of the archway, which was now but a wooden cradle supported on two pillars of stone. Renith, Old Wobbly, Uilig, and Roben leaned their shoulders against their target shields as two dozen attackers maintained the assault on the gap in the town wall. Rig's curved tower shield could not fit into the groove in the stones, so he had placed it furthest forward so that when pushed back it would be supported by the shields on either side. The defenders met each successive wave of attack, stabbing over or under their targets' curving edges. They aimed for ankles, feet, hands or faces. They felt the press of a second line of Darnok behind them, lending them weight and protecting them with target shields held above their heads. The attackers launched themselves again and again at this narrow shield wall from the rubble, dodging the stabbing spears coming at them through the murder holes, bringing down axes with all their strength so as to pry the defences apart or stave in an ill-protected head should the swing knock aside a weakly held shield. Old Wobbly took a cut through the leather armour on his left shoulder, but he held the line and stabbed his attacker's forearm. Uilig felt a blaze of pain shoot through his ear and then warm wetness spill down his cheek; he gnashed his teeth, leaned back into his shield and stabbed his dirk into a boot that showed beneath his shield. The line between the pillars held … for the moment.

Knab had joined the defences by then, as had anyone else who had attended the moot unarmed. He leapt up onto the wall a dozen paces to the south of the archway and he bellowed a challenge at Sokaroth. The rival chieftain could hardly refuse and he bashed his way through the flood of surging men to get at his enemy. Ah, but there were other chieftains, too, who had risen to their positions by daring, by offering and accepting duels, and by winning all their fights. Hargar Sodargen of the Ilkaren Clan from Maddersfjord was nearby and he pounced on the opportunity to claim the life of the famous Knab Sokilg. Sodargen ordered his men aside and surged towards the wall.

That was when Kyre pulled the lever connected to the trap door covering a concealed pit outside the wall. Kyre was no warrior and would never anchor a shield wall, indeed, the prospect of battle terrified him. But Lora's mother, Loska, had pulled the bard from the roundhouse when Rolf had first raised the alarm and she had put him in charge of the lever. Loska's choice was a wise one, for he could pull a lever, and his sense of timing was well-honed. And of course Knab had not randomly selected his place along the wall to issue his challenge, he had set himself directly in front of that pit outside the wall. Kyre pulled the lever and the ground fell out from under Sodargen and a half-dozen other men close to the wall. Spikes at the bottom of the pit broke the men's fall, gravel from the beach fell in on top of them, as did a few of their comrades in arms. The screaming unnerved the attackers and made many retreat a few paces from the pit. That was when Knab signalled for the archers to get to work. A good three-score archers - nigh on a third of Krannogberg's defenders - rose from behind the wall and loosed arrows into the throng of attackers. In such close quarters and with the attackers packed together, the archers could hardly miss. From the step of the roundhouse, Lora loosed a pair of arrows, smacking them off a merlon and an iron helmet respectively.

Two volleys flew out before Sokaroth managed to rally the Jarlags and their allies for a renewed attack on the wall in other places where the archers were not so numerous. His men were undisciplined and unused to such a well-organized defence, but they had their blood up and they were brave. Sokaroth had enough men at his disposal to maintain a strong attack over the rubble in front of the gap in the wall, as well as to make two thrusts against the wall a dozen paces to the north and south of the gap. The fight south of the archway was a near thing. The attackers braved the arrows, crossed the ditch and gained the wall. Instead of throwing themselves against it, trying to clamber between the merlons, they formed a protective roof with their shields, giving themselves a safe enclave behind the shoulder-tall wall from which to launch a concerted attack. Under that roof, the attackers built two broad steps made from the shields of fallen warriors, piled one on top of the other. When they were ready, those warriors holding their shields aloft to form the roof pulled back and let other attackers scramble up the steps and onto the wall.

The first Jarlag over the wall tumbled onto the end of a spear, but the second got a foot onto a merlon and jumped over the defenders, flopping to the ground behind the line of Krannogbergers. The man didn't last long because a shield wench lodged a hand axe in his helmet, but the tactic startled the Krannogbergers and they did not react quickly enough to it to prevent the next dozen attackers from leaping among them.

As the line of defenders fell into a pitched, confused fight with the first Jarlags over the wall, Loska ordered the reserve - thirty Darnok, all well-trained in the shield wall - to contain the attack. The reserve crashed into the battle, and the Jarlags found themselves trapped between an advancing crescent of shields in front of them and the stone wall behind. Many a Darnok were trapped as well, and as the shield wall compressed the confused mêlée, those blessed by Florri found themselves on the roundhouse side of the struggle and were pulled to safety; those Jarlags in similar positions were sent to Hondrig for His final judgement. Sokaroth's warriors found themselves forced backwards towards the perimeter wall foot by bloody foot, and had no chance to form their own shield wall.

Meanwhile, at the archway, where the Ilkaren continued to scramble over the rubble and confront Rig's shield wall, the defenders held steady. Darnok spears stabbed out from the murder holes on either side of the gap in the wall, wounding attackers on the flanks of the attack, or driving them back, preventing them from overwhelming the defence with superior numbers. The Darnok defenders even flung the Ilkaren dead on top of their brothers, so that the pile of rubble grew more cluttered and harder to scale, though the blank, lifeless eyes of dead friends likely did more to dull the Ilkaren attack than Krannogberg's defences.

Further north, on the far side of the archway, the Jorgor still attacked the wall, though they found it angrily defended and they could not clear it. Isolated attackers, seeking to seize

Karn's attention and receive Her holy blessing, not to mention glory for their reputations, darted away from the main thrusts of the battle and tried to scale the wall where defenders did not cluster behind the stone barrier. The Krannogbergers were not so numerous that they could post defenders along the full perimeter of the wall, so Loska had to dispatch shield wenches in threes to repel these attacks. Thus the Darnok, though outnumbered nigh on three to one, maintained a dangerous, fragile balance against the attackers.

Inside the town, where Sokaroth's raiders had cleared the wall, some raiders surged outwards against the ends of the crescent-shaped shield wall, trying to slip around it or force it back from the outer wall. The attack on the left of the advancing semi-circle was savage and the Darnok there could not hold their formation, but for the moment other Krannogbergers managed to deal with the odd attacker who slipped containment. A few Jarlags managed to lunge over-top the closing shield wall, hoping again to cause havoc from behind, but those attackers were beset by the shield wenches and thus could not turn to attack the backs of the men they had just cleared.

Rigald Sokaroth was as crafty a chieftain as Knab, and though he was well pleased that his attackers had taken the fight over the wall, in addition to his considerable numerical advantage he had other plans to overwhelm his Darnok enemies. While the struggle at the outer wall continued and the attention of the defenders, including the reserve, was fixed on the fighting underway, a final enemy boat put ashore at the far end of the strand. It was a small boat, and thus slower, so the plan had always been that it could deliver a late, unexpected blow. No one was there to resist the arrival of a final thirty Jarlag attackers except Rolf, leading a half-dozen shaggy followers. The Jarlag orders were not to join the main assault, but to skirt the village and come at the perimeter wall from behind, from the east, where they guessed there might be another gate opening into the town. They scattered those few dogs who harried their arrival and jogged around the beached Darnok longboats without anyone but the village curs noticing.

Rolf and his small pack followed them, raising Skalagg, the Netherworld, with their barking. Climbing up the path to the redoubt, Ellena, Thay's sister, noticed the ruckus and sprinted up the short final ascent to the refuge. She alerted Kargar, the old caretaker of the redoubt, who not only lived in the cave with the savage cats but who also commanded the shifts of young lads who employed the fire arrows. Kargar had heard the din but the mist and rain had obscured any sight of the fjord or of the town and so he had no idea what was going on. When he heard Ellena's news, he ordered the two young men with him to shoot blazing arrows down into the back paddock - the sward above the tide at the foot of the fjord that the Darnok had walled off long ago with stones. As the attackers rounded the town's beached longboats along the strand, warning beacons started dropping from the sky, one of which brought down in blind luck the leader of the surprise attack.

Thay, standing ready with buckets of water and his rake inside the wall, behind the town's roundhouse, saw the fire arrows out of the corner of his eye. He would never have noticed had his mind not been brooding on the attack and Sokaroth's tactics; surely the place to attack was the place where no Darnok protected the wall. He had kept his eyes on the east wall, behind the village, and thus he saw the fire arrows dropping into the back paddock. He darted inside the back door of town's main hall, sped around the fire pit at its centre and alerted Lora's mother. When Loska heard Thay's warning, she sprang to the back doorway of the roundhouse. She whistled loudly, drawing the attention of the goodwives in the roundhouse, and yelled, "Get the shield wenches to the back wall!" The Jarlags were jogging across a last open space before the wall.

Loska dashed to the point of attack, longspear at the ready. She was not alone; Lars, Lora, and Thay joined her. The first man to try the wall got Loska's spear driven into his shoulder and he fell back screaming. Thay also drove a man back with a spear, and Lora finally scored a hit, an arrow to the shoulder throwing a Jarlag from the wall. It was hardly enough, however, as the wave of the other attackers crashed upon the defence, with a half-dozen men clambering up to the merlons unopposed. Lars yelled, rushed forward and, mustering every ounce of his strength, swung at one with *Harbinger*. Although awkward in his swing - the blade was too big for a boy his age - Lars nevertheless managed to drive the rusty blade into the man's left leg and send him flying off the wall. The next five attackers hesitated, not because of a young lad who had flopped to his knees holding a claymore, but because they saw a new defender facing them.

Magon, the Priest of Hondrig, rushed in front of the attackers, his arms held wide and high, pulling the folds of his pale cloak and robes apart. His flowing white hair and beard all gave him the appearance of some ferocious white eagle protecting its eyrie. "Hold!" he yelled, his most commanding voice filling the misty air. "Hold for your own sakes! This land is warded! Hold lest you wish that on every new moon a *bjerndyr* stalk your children! On Even Day and on the night of the winter solstice, the werebear will bring misery to your kin!" Then, to the astonishment of the attackers, he thrust out his arms again and blood exploded across the ground inside the wall before him ... and where it touched the ground, it formed the bloody shape of an ice bear. "Behold the *bjerndyr*!"

The attackers stopped and gawked at the priest - now suddenly brandishing aloft a *Valknut*, Heligat's holy symbol of three intertwined triangles that all men know draws Her gaze. Terror halted them, for priests manipulate the magic of the Gods. They cast fearful eyes at the bloody bear shape. "Go! You still may escape the curse! Go now!"

The men hesitated, all but one. The largest of the attackers, a giant of a man stripped to the waist and in the grip of a frenzy let loose a horn blast of a bellow. He leapt up onto the wall in a whirlwind of dirty blonde hair, spittle spilling from his mouth onto his bushy beard. His eyes were wide and wild, he carried no shield, and he brandished a large two-handed axe that he pulled back over his head.

"Hold!" Magon yelled again, though his voice betrayed a hint of fear that he was facing a man blessed by Karn and converted into one of Her berserkers of legend. Some of the Jarlags surged back onto the wall, and Magon, seeing this and fearing disaster, cried again, "The Curse!"

In that moment, when the courage of the Jarlags had rallied, the Curse struck; an arrow slammed through the eye of the frenzied man and punched out the back of his skull. His axe dropped from his hands at the top of his backswing. He screamed, twisted, and dropped. The other attackers, their courage balanced on a dirk edge, promptly lost heart and jumped back off the wall. Rather than struggle against the Gods, whose intervention they had surely witnessed, they fled, circled south of the village and joined their comrades on the beach.

As the Jarlags retreated, Magon exhaled a deep breath and looked around. His eyes met Loska's, who brushed a strand of her brown hair away from her face and managed a smile. "My daughter makes good arrows, and she can shoot them."

Loska turned and ordered Thay and Lars to keep the watch over the back wall before sending the spear maidens back through the roundhouse. Then she grabbed Lora by the arm and said, "You! Come with me."

Back at the one struggle inside the curtain wall, where Sokaroth's men faced the constricting shield wall, the fight had become a horror of shit, corpses, blood, and gore. The Jarlags had managed to get a score of men over the wall by this time and had finally pulled themselves into a shield wall of their own, albeit a shorter one than that of the defenders, which still curled around them. Their objective was simply to hold firm the space that they had carved open giving time for more men to join them. Those men locked their shields over the heads of those in front of them, forming a protective carapace like that of the tortoise. They thus protected the men in front from the overhead axe swings so dangerous to the cohesion of the wall. But still Jarlags fell as swords stabbed between the gaps of the shields, cut their legs or found gaps between their armour. Krannogberger women hauled their wounded back to the roundhouse while the Jarlags struggled to pull their own wounded out from under their feet. The training of the Darnok proved itself and the defenders inched forward, constricting Sokaroth's men into a tighter and tighter bind with every advance.

Knab himself finally tipped the delicate balance of the battle. He had been fighting by the rubble of the archway, bellowing for Sokaroth to fight him, but his rival had withdrawn to size up the state of the attack. At length Knab did the same, spotting the struggle going on inside the walls to the south of the gap. He called to Tharnil and pointed to the roof of the roundhouse. "Get archers up there shooting into that mass beyond the wall!" Then he grabbed two archers and two shield wenches with spears and pointed. "You two," he said to the women, pointing at the merlons between the archway and where the Jarlags had made it across the wall, "use your spears to force men back from that part of the wall. You two," he said to the archers, "make sure anyone who comes at me gets an arrow in the head. Go!"

The women drove forward and thrust their spears at the Jarlags surging at the wall south of the gap. Knab sprang up on top of the wall and dashed along its length, one foot landing on every other merlon. One Jarlag outside the wall lunged forward to drive his spear at the Darnok chieftain, but two arrows slammed into the spearman, throwing him back. Knab bellowed and launched himself through the air and onto the backs of the Jarlags in the shield wall inside the town, knocking them to the ground and blowing apart their defensive organization.

The Krannogbergers immediately surrounded and cut-off the separated bits of the enemy, stabbing and slashing, advancing, and stabbing and slashing again. Knab scrambled to his feet and turned himself into a screaming demon, freed from the bounds of a disciplined fight. His axe flew left, right and overhead, causing panic behind the lines of attackers. Then it was a question of taking down the slowest of those who fled back over the wall.

Tharnil had placed a dozen archers on the roof of the roundhouse and they fired into the Jarlags still on the far side of the wall. For those raiders, the flight of their comrades back across the wall and the rain of arrows undermined their resolve and they pulled back to the shingle beach. Rigald Sokaroth, seeing his men retreat from the wall, made a virtue of necessity, ordering all the attackers back, rallying them into a broad shield wall, three deep, which allowed them cover from the volleys of arrows coming from the archers on the roof of the roundhouse and from behind the perimeter wall. Behind that imposing protective barrier, the Jarlags and their allies took their time to build a fire, light fire arrows of their own, and shoot them at the Darnok roundhouse and cottages. Soon Loska and the other women, as well as Lars, Lora, and Thay, were all frantically pulling burning shingles down from the roofs with their hoes or dousing what fires had caught with bucketfuls of water drawn from the well. The drizzle of earlier in the day was giving way to patches of blue sky, but many of the shingles were damp, so the fires did not spread as Sokaroth had hoped. No defender was positioned to protect the town's boats, however, and the arrows soon had fires building in all the longboats and in the fishing boats. Smoke billowed from the town, blown on the driving wind up the Andersfjord.

Then the Jarlags piled masses of seaweed and driftwood on their fire, and pulled their shield wall back behind the blaze. Soon the fire cast its own billowing smoke towards the town and its defenders. When the driftwood was firmly afire, some pieces as long as a man and weighing as much as two, the attackers readied themselves. They threw a final pile of seaweed on the fire, enveloping the town's archway in smoke, and then they attacked. The shield wall pulled apart as the men surged forward, casting flaming brands of driftwood at the defences under the arch. It took three men to haul the largest piece of burning driftwood up over the piles of stone and bodies in front of the archway and then hoist it at the defenders, but they managed the feat, hurling the larger part of a trunk of a tree against the shields blocking the entrance to Krannogberg. The trunk acted like a battering ram. It slammed against the shield barrier and despite grooves and blocks of wood propping up the shields, it knocked Rig, Renith, Old Wobbly, Uilig, and Roben all back away from the gap.

Jarlag, Ilkaren, and Jorgor attackers poured through the opening. Knab had just enough time to trigger his last trap, the caltrops. When he saw the men rushing the archway with the huge piece of driftwood, he signalled to Kyre and the bard upended the large jute sack containing clusters of long, narrow nails forged together in such a manner that regardless of how they came to rest, two or three spikes would protrude into the air. The caltrops spilled in front of the archway and again the first wave of attackers fared poorly, receiving many injuries. But the attackers pushed past their fallen comrades, shields held high to protect them from the arrows pouring into them. They surged into the town with a great roar of triumph.

Standing against them was Krannogberg's last defence, Knab's depleted reserve force drawn into a shield wall. Knab barked orders at the Darnok, ordering them to attach themselves to each end of the wall, expanding it. Then he roared a challenge and drove his men at the attack. The attackers could not get over the rubble, the dead and injured, the caltrops, and the burning driftwood in good order, they could only surge through in a fury of confusion. So the Darnok had the advantage of discipline when their shield wall careened into the ragged attacking wave. And they had long practiced the shield wall, forming two compact lines, the ones behind hoisting their shields to protect the heads and backs of the men in the front line. Shield wenches jabbed overtop the wall with their longspears. The attacks to that point had been vicious, but there were still near a gross of defenders putting up determined resistance. Knab himself was a spinning devil of axe blades slicing at the invaders.

Sokaroth threw more men through the archway. The defenders weren't numerous enough to hem the attackers in and many of Sokaroth's men got around the edges of the shield wall and started looting the cottages. In the end their greed was a mistake, for had they attacked the back of the shield wall, they might have shattered it. But many of those men were Ilkaren and Jorgor, who did not have the same hatred of the Darnok that the Jarlags kept burning in their hearts. Instead, these men did as many Fjordlanders did, they sought what pillage they could and placed less value on the thoroughness of the victory. They ransacked a half-dozen cottages before the tide of the battle turned again.

Ultimately, what broke the attack was the clearing weather and the opportunity that it afforded Kargar, the caretaker in the redoubt, to rain fire arrows down on the enemy longboats, which he could now finally see. Sokaroth had convinced the Ilkaren and Jorgor chieftains to follow him, but the pact could survive neither the much more determined resistance than was promised nor the danger of losing their longboats. The Jarlag allies would not accept the unappetizing prospect of being stranded in the Andersfjord or having to lug their loot overland for days, all the while at the mercy of any parties of revenge-seeking Krannogbergers harrying them on their way home. Hargar Sodargen of the Ilkaren was already dead and Big Erig Somardin of the Jorgor was ill-inclined to see his vessel go up in flames. When the fire arrows landed in his boat, he pulled back a score of men to extinguish the fires. The other captains took note of Somardin's order and then they noticed the flames catching in their own vessels. Big Erig saw that the attack was petering out and he blew the retreat on his horn.

That horn blast drove a dagger through the last chance of keeping up the attack. Sokaroth screamed in frustration, but he knew he could not press any further. In the end he had no option but to order his Jarlags back to the boats. Even the retreat was hard. The Darnok kept shooting their arrows and the steady trickle of fire arrows from the redoubt ensured that the Jarlag crews had to fight fires as well as launch their ships into the Andersfjord while avoiding getting hit.

The raid was a severe setback for the Jarlags. Instead of a glorious victory with plunder of silver and slaves, they had nothing to show for their efforts but a haul of sorrow. They lost a hundred men, between death and capture, another two dozen returned to Sangspit maimed, and no spoils went with them to pay *lifgyld* to the families of the dead. To maintain his chieftainship, Sokaroth had to dig deeply into his own wealth to compensate many families, though only if they supported him in the face of two challenges to his leadership that came subsequently from disgruntled rivals. The Ilkaren lost their chieftain and nearly three score clansmen besides, though some of the survivors returned with loot enough to dull the memory of the bloody Darnok resistance. The Jorgor, too, paid a heavy price, forty-eight men dead and one longboat lost to fire arrows. They did not craft any ballads commemorating the sacrifice of their warriors that day.

For all that the attackers suffered, the Darnok victory was a pyrrhic one. Of the town's nine score warriors and shield wenches, thirty-four died that day or succumbed to their wounds over the weeks that followed. Another two score were wounded, eighteen severely enough that they could not work for the rest of the season, and some half-dozen were disabled for life. The Darnok turned the roundhouse into a house of healing and many worked tirelessly with Torga Danail to tend to the wounded, though that time they spent was lost on the usual labours of the community, which centred on preparing the town for the winter. Over those days, Lora absorbed more of Krannogberg's healing lore than she had hitherto learnt in all her short life.

Magon conducted burial ceremonies and sang the *Cleaving Rite* for the next two weeks as new cairns sprang up on the middle vale. The families who passed the summer up on the ranges of the plateau and the foothills of the Boldring Mountains soon heard of the attack and returned to Krannogberg in a rage. Leigh, Cairn's father, was incensed to behold the damage in his town; eight cottages completely destroyed and another half-dozen badly damaged. Also destroyed were all of Krannogberg's boats, a disaster for a town that needed to fish to live. But even the most bitter of the Darnok knew that they could do nothing to exact revenge from the Jarlags. They had a new fight on their hands, survival in the face of the coming winter.

Knab and the richest of the others still alive pooled their resources. They traded goods and silver for two longboats and a half-dozen fishing boats from Narhaven and the other villages on the Bight, though they balked at the price their neighbours demanded. They paid but they remembered. They had captured thirteen enemy and they put these men to work in chains, repairing the damaged cottages and building what new ones could be constructed before the Sea Wolves came in the early autumn. It was a blessing when the Sea Wolves accepted the captives in place of a tithe, for the Darnok would have been hard placed to part from any of their grain, meat or fish. The straits of the town were dire enough that no Sea Wolves decided to muster out in Krannogberg that year, bringing no much needed new wealth to the community.

It was the first battle that Lora, Lars, and Thay had witnessed. Cairn pressed them, begging them to tell the tale, but the scale of Krannogberg's misery held their tongues. He got the story from Kyre, who was accustomed to setting even bitter tragedy to verse, but only when the rest of the Krannogbergers did, as a dirge sung at that year's sombre Hearthfire celebration.

Rolf the Steadfast lived long enough to enjoy a place of honour at that modest feast thanking the Gods for the bounty enjoyed by the Darnok, such as it was that year. He was given a cushion on which to lie at the foot of Knab's chair and he was given choice morsels of meat. Not only had he helped save the village, but he had attached himself to the most seriously wounded in aftermath of the battle, greeting them when they woke in the morning and curling up beside them as night fell on the roundhouse. Just before midwinter, the old dog died. He was laid to rest in his own cairn in the middle vale set on a spot with a good view of the Bight. With Magon and Kyre's permission, as Knab laid the last stone upon the small pile of rocks, Lars sang the entire *Cleaving Rite* in his fair voice, all one hundred and one verses of it.

For Darknight, at midwinter, as he turned thirteen, Lars composed his first verse. It was a lament in Rolf's honour that worked itself into the legends of the Darnok:

A noble hound, who never let us down,
*   a worthy guard of honour.*
One loyal dog, undaunted by the fog,
*   shall guard our shores forever.*

The puppies Rolf had sired down through the years all rose in general esteem.

And yet, for all their hardship that winter, every Krannogberger paid due respect to Florri, the God of Good Fortune, who controls the whims of luck, as they did to Knab;

for while Florri must surely have blessed them, they also knew that their chieftain's preparations had saved them. They also sent prayers of thanks to the long departed soul of Helgya Darik. For had her verse and Rig's remembering it not brought the Darnok to the roundhouse that misty afternoon, and had the verse's warning of danger not caused many of the folk to be dressed for battle, they knew their fate might have resembled that of their distant kin in Jorrumsfjord, destruction and enslavement to the Jarlags.

Part II

The Tithe of the Sea Wolves

Chapter One

On a misty autumn afternoon two moons prior to the youngsters' sixteenth birthing day, Cairn and his mother, Fallig, returned from the plateau. They rode their shaggy ponies behind their sheep and cattle, accompanied by their dogs, two flanking the livestock and one driving it down the track. Oddly, Leigh did not ride alongside his wife and son. Fallig's neighbours helped her settle the livestock into one of the back paddocks. Lora was out on her dory crabbing on the Bight, but Thay and Lars ran to help their friend Cairn round up and direct the cattle. Lars overheard Fallig respond to a question from Aganas and he shot Thay an excited look.

"What?" Thay asked, furrowing his brow in puzzlement.

"We're to go up!" Lars gushed, his ice-blue eyes alight with excitement.

"Up where?"

Lars broke into a chant:

> *Above the shore   the slopes soar up.*
> *Brood below moon,   under sun loom.*
> *Glowing with snow: cold and remote.*
> *Naught escapes frost;   even thought cannot.*
>
> *Here Norrgi hawks   His frigid spite-spit,*
> *blowing His bone-dust,   throwing His water-rocks.*
>
> *Fjordlander!   Oars are your lore;*
> *anchors and anvils,   angst-bound anglers.*
> *You birth brine-riders,   tide-readers and bards.*
> *Come not here now;   none shall live long.*

Thay arched an eyebrow at Cairn.

Cairn ignored him and gave a last smack to the hindquarters of a hairy brown cow, sending it trotting through the paddock gateway. The big lad couldn't manage a straight face for long, though, before wiggling his eyebrows and grinning.

"Yes!" Lars cried, shaking clenched fists in triumph above his head.

As Fallig closed and barred the wooden gate with a loop of rope, Lora's stern mother, Loska, planted herself in front of Lars and poked him in the chest. "Don't get too excited, youngling. You'll work harder at the foot of yon mountains than you ever have during a winter down here. And don't think you can get away with anything with my Lora, just because she's out of my sight. Fallig can skin you just as well as I can."

And with those words hanging in the air as Loska walked off, Lars and Thay shuffled uncomfortably. Their glances suddenly revealed more sheepishness than excitement. Cairn looked from one to the other, wondering what he hadn't caught - though he did catch Lars' new conceit; a single braid of his white-blonde hair dangling in front of the left ear past the temple.

What Thay knew that Cairn didn't was that Lars had other conceits, trying to contrive greater time alone with Lora over the summer: offering to help her with her brewing, though she had retorted she needed no help in lugging sacks of barley; volunteering to row her dory out to her crabbing grounds, though she had declared that she could row better than he; and, insisting on helping her strengthen her spear work, though she had promptly knocked his father's too-large helmet off his head with her spear.

Thay had noticed, and struggled greatly with the resultant roiling in his stomach. At first he had tried imposing his own presence on the brewing, crabbing, and spear work, eliciting an encouraging, exciting response from Lora, though an opposite one from Lars. This had both pleased and disturbed him deeply, but then he perceived certain inescapable facts; Lora could indeed lug her own sacks of grains, pull oars with better coordination than anyone, and crack her spear against Thay's ribs more often than he could against hers. When he rowed out alone at the end of the summer days to haul in the nets - a job his father now entrusted fully to the youngster - he pondered this apparent discrepancy, but he soon discovered another quandary to consider ... Lora offering to help him with the rowing and hauling. Alas for Thay's soaring heart, that only happened once before Lars insisted on coming along.

And then, after a few days, the two lads had to scowl together across the Andersfjord at the dory of the older, handsomer Dag Somorgin, who sat at the prow laughing, rare sunlight refracting off his blonde head of hair as Lora pulled on the oars, rowing off to retrieve his father's nets. That situation might have driven both the young boys mad had the Black Wolves clan of the Sea Wolves not come the very next week and taken Dag off as their annual tithe.

Cairn had missed all these new complexities, but over the next few days of preparation for the winter, seemed to settle into the middle of them effortlessly. Whatsoever task assigned to Lora - loading crates with smoked flounder or herring, preserving autumn fruits, or, selecting replacement spear shafts - Cairn, too, found a way of doing his own assigned task in the same place. Thay just shook his head when he presented himself at his last afternoon of Straelish practice with Aganas before they headed up onto the plateau, only to find that Cairn and Lars had suddenly taken an interest in learning the language, an interest he normally only shared with Lora. He felt anger towards his friends, guilt over feeling such anger, something heady and unknown whenever Lora smiled at him, as well as deep confusion, for Lora would sometimes seek out Cairn's help re-stitching a buckskin coat, or Lars' songs when loading the cart with coal, or his own eye for a straight line when fletching.

One blustery morn, Fallig inspected the pair of carts, nodded in satisfaction, and pointed for Thay to get up to drive the second, knowing him to be the poorest rider. She drove the first and the other three youngsters had ponies to take them up to the hills. Lars, Lora, and Thay nearly forgot to wave back to their kin as they departed town.

It was a harsh season, but not so bad as the tales would have led them to believe; most local bears were hibernating and none of the ice bears came down from the north, the snow was plentiful but the bitterest cold was rare, and the Tears of the Ghosts fell only thrice. Despite the relatively tame conditions, they soon discovered the cold that bites through layers of skins and woollens to gnaw at the bones. During the long nights running up to their birthday, they would do some weapons practice in the barn under Leigh's eye - axes and shields, though Cairn also used his maul, *Orgor's Awl* - and after that, they would huddle in the cottage learning to craft themselves snowshoes, spinning wool, or fletching replacement arrows for Fallig and Lora, who kept the barn rafters well-stocked with venison, fowl or snow hare. Lars provided them a measure of gaiety on those dark nights by playing some of Kyre's songs on his bone flute.

By day, prior to the first snowfalls, Leigh had them collect bog ore from around the heath and bring it back to the small furnace he had dug into an earth bank behind the barn. Lars, Lora, and Thay watched Leigh and Cairn smelt the bog ore into iron, using large quantities of black spruce for the fire. As the days got colder and the snow arrived, he had them chop down trees in a stand of woods northeast of the cottage, at the very feet of the mountains, though they only felled those he said were suitable for shipbuilding. When the worst of the winter hit them, Leigh had them out more, not less, and often overnighting in lean-tos that he showed them how to build. Cairn's father made them work with the shaggy horses to drag back over the snows the logs they had felled earlier in the autumn on a sleigh they had built themselves under Fallig's watchful eye. Cairn's mother took them far beyond the little lake in front of the cottage to fish, or ice fish, as the season drew on. When a particularly bad storm hit, Leigh had them work in the little barn, hewing off branches, squaring off the logs, and stacking them for transport in the spring. While Cairn's father couldn't shoot a bow very well, he could lay snares and he showed them how to read tracks that revealed where martens or snow hares passed.

They worked harder than they ever had before during winter, but they enjoyed themselves, especially after the end of autumn, when dreary rain gave way to the bright glimmering of snowfall. They got a surprise not long after, on the eve of Darknight. For the winter solstice, Fallig took them snowshoeing down towards the fjord. When they had dropped low enough, the snow in the valley of the Tallog River gave way to green grasses. They strapped their snowshoes to their backs and hiked down the boggy slopes to the long, narrow lake, the Tallogswater. Nightfall saw them skirting its northern shore, nearing the lake's western outflow. As they approached that point where the Tallog River resumed its march to the fjord, they detected lights ahead of them, and soon enough they could see the glimmering shafts of a campfire and lanterns. They crossed a final ridge and came down into a camp set up at the edge of the hot springs that bubbled from the earth, and in the camp were the other mothers, Rena, Loska, and Thülla.

The women stripped down, and, ordered the striplings out of their clothes and into the hot springs. When they hesitated, Thülla stepped forward, fists planted firmly on her bare hips, "Sure, you've all done nothing but dream of seeing naked bodies over this last year, here's your chance. Take a gander! This is the body I live in and that bore Ellena and you, Thay. You see, we're here tonight to celebrate your turning sixteen. You'll be adults soon enough, and Lora's already in the midst of her change into womanhood; what's likely had you all at odds and ends this past year. That's fine. It's natural. But you're all, at furthest, second cousins once removed. We take our spouses from other settlements, and sometimes go live there, to make sure that our mate in life isn't family. So recognize the feelings you're feeling for what they are! Cravings for celebrating and creating life. All that will come in due course. But just as you're able to control your urges when you look on us, your mothers, you can control your urges as they relate to other Darnok girls," and then with a glance at Lora, "and boys, until you meet others from away."

Thay did take a gander, and he saw his mother differently. She stood tall, taller than anyone else present, and she was slim. Her normally amber hair - currently darker owing to its wetness - hung down to the small of her back, making her seem taller yet. Thay suddenly understood that his notion of a muscled person had always had a man as its avatar; his mother was in good shape, the muscles of her legs and arms well defined, and she carried no excess bulk. Her piercing grey eyes gave her a stern aspect. When he looked at her small breasts and the matting of hair at her groin, he found nothing strange happened to him; Hondrig did not bring the world to an end, Zareth did not make him feel lustful, and Tanat did not make anything stick out at right angles. Her body was human, and normal, for all that it was strange to him.

He spared a glance for Loska and his new concept of "muscular" solidified. She had been a spear wench and had always commanded Krannogberg's defences whenever Knab travelled or walked the Darnok lands. She was the embodiment of the Holy Karn from Kyre's sagas, the striding Goddess of War who had famously hurled a spear over the Boldring Mountains to kill Sk'van's earthly body and banish him to Skalagg. He didn't doubt that Loska could hurl a spear a great distance, or stab it clear through any raider who might come down on Krannogberg on a dark night.

His mother interrupted his thoughts by declaring, "Now! The lecture's over. Get your clothes off and join us in the springs!"

And thus they peeled off their woollens, skins, and coats, with the lads perhaps allowing themselves a peek at Lora's ripening body, and Lora certainly appearing to reciprocate. Despite the dawning of his new understanding, Thay still wasn't sure about controlling his urges where Lora was concerned, and so he scrambled over the rocks and into the warm pools in the stream as quickly as he could. Despite his worries, he soon lost himself in the revelry of the moment, as they spent their birthday frolicking in the jagged rock rills and shallow pools of steaming water. Lora cut her backside on the stone and cursed. Despite the earlier lecture, Thülla had to shoo off Lars when he offered to tend to the cut, though it wasn't serious and they laughed at the foolishness. The women had brought a keg of Lora's beer and, once tapped, it proved a wondrously cold, refreshing brew, that tasted of juniper berries roasted in freshly baked bread. After the first round of bathing, when they sat pleasantly shivering on stones beside the pools - Thay noting that while some things shrivelled up in the cold air, other things popped out! - Loska lifted her cup and declared, "Rulla hear us! We pray You keep this young woman and these young men under Your wise eye! Skol!" And with that she downed her cup and, laughing, scrambled into the rocky pools again.

§

In the following spring, after the youths had returned from their winter on the plateau, Leigh took the decision to end the annual rite of melancholy that came with separating Cairn from the other three youngsters for the summer. He decided that Cairn, rather than going back up onto the plateau with the livestock, should stay behind and learn something of the sea. He bade Fallig spend more time with her son than was usual during the spring thaw and then he took to going with the large lad to the Harrowood for long talks about everything and nothing at all. Cairn did not resent the time away from his friends, for he knew that he would finally spend a summer with them, far from the heather, the blasting wind, and the blasted sheep of the Boldring Mountains. Finally, when the snows had retreated enough in the face of rains and fair winds, Leigh and Fallig closed up the winter barn, loaded up their horse cart, and gathered together their animals. They said a long farewell to Cairn and set off across the plateau, Fallig weeping all the way up the fjord.

Cairn stayed with Rig and Thülla - sharing a bed with Thay - but crewed the boat of Renith and Lars. It did not take long for him to dislike being on the water. At first, Renith was eager to have Cairn's bulk to haul in the nets, but the big youth had a miserable time finding his sea legs. Every time he pulled on a line, he either pulled the gunnel down to the waterline or cast himself into the Andersfjord. Cairn squawked so much about his regular dips in the fjord that Lars openly called into doubt Cairn's oft repeated claims that he could swim the length of the Tallogswater twice in the time it took to shear a sheep.

Renith and Cairn finally settled on an unstated understanding. Each morning Renith would search until he could find the slightest thing that needed doing on shore, whereupon he would curse and loudly proclaim that he could not take the boat out for the day's fishing. Cairn would then graciously volunteer to do whatever needed doing in order to allow Renith and Lars to lay down the nets. Renith would exclaim that he could not possibly leave such a difficult task to one man alone. Cairn would stoically wave away any such concerns, stating that hard work was oft lonely work up in the hills and that he was used to it. Renith would sigh and thank Cairn before taking Lars and putting the boat into the fjord. Lars would look to the sky and, regardless of whatever the skies held in portent, would say, "Thank you, Norrgi, for keeping me dry today."

Whenever she did not accompany her father Uilig out fishing, Lora would speed through her chores and then join Cairn in his daily task on shore. Although Cairn became the subject of Lars' lighthearted jabbing, both Lars and Thay were jealous of Cairn's time ashore in Lora's company. Even Rig felt jealousy tug at him when he saw Renith and Rena's lintel sanded and painted, the stones of the back paddock rebuilt, and fresh shingles put on the roof of their house.

Cairn and Lora worked harder than they ever had before, but Cairn was never heard complaining after his last sodden jaunt in Renith's fishing boat. And yet, for all the joy the four adolescents had at their first summer together, the boys sensed a change come over Lora. Even during their happiest moments together, a sadness would creep into her eyes and she would grow quiet and pensive. The boys knew her well enough to know that she was working some problem over in her mind.

§

Then one day a moon after Brightnight, the summer solstice, the Sea Wolves returned to Krannogberg. Three great long-boats slid into Hondrig's Bight on a bright summer day. The water was still and reflected the brilliant sky like a polished silver shield. Hardly a whiff of air stirred between the walls of the Andersfjord and the folk had already peeled off their vests and unbuttoned their shirts in the unusual heat. The first hint of danger came when horns sounded from the watchtower that served both Narhaven and Krannogberg. Uilig ran to the roundhouse and sounded the horn there. A few boats fishing the fjord rowed to shore in time for their men to grab their arms, but those in the Bight were easily outpaced by the longboats with their great rack of oars stroking the water in perfect unison.

Knab ordered a defence prepared, so Cairn joined the shield wall for the first time, feeling alone despite the other warriors, for his friends were all out on their fishing dories. But the Sea Wolves did not come to pillage. Summer had been good to the Arctic Wolves. Seven men had paid their *lifgylds* and the clan could buy fitting hospitality in Sagear's Cove with the Higgersuld without the need to spill any blood. Kindron Sopallig, the grizzled Sea Wolf captain out of whose service the Darnok chieftain had mustered some fifteen years earlier, had repaired his boats, polished his mail, and sharpened the blades of his axe. What he needed in Krannogberg was not stores for a trip across the sea, but strong bodies to fill the gaps of the departed men. He had hung a shield from his mast before making his way first to Narhaven. While they gathered up two lads from the village up the coast, Krannogberg's fishing boats rowed ashore, including those of Uilig, Rig, and Renith. Lora, Thay, and Lars spilled from their fathers' boats in a whirlwind of flailing limbs and ran for their leathers, weapons, and target shields. Lars brought out *Harbinger* and hung it over his back, and he made sure his father's metal helm didn't prevent his plait of white-blonde hair from dangling past his temple.

The realization spread amongst the Darnok that, with this Sea Wolf visit, the time had come for Lars, Thay, and Cairn to leave Krannogberg. A great many wondered how the three young men would fit in with their new clan; they also wondered how Lora would take being left behind - for the first time ever. The lads, too, bubbled with excitement, because selection by the Sea Wolves, for all it meant gruelling work and servitude, was a rite of passage into manhood.

Three longboats finally hove around Hargur's Head and entered the Andersfjord. They made good speed on the water, and their bare masts looked like claws reaching to the God-space. When they slid ashore, Kindron Sopallig dropped down from the prow of his ship, his bulk sinking into the pebbly beach. The years had not changed him much; his chest still appeared hewn from stone, his blue eyes danced with a fiery joy, and his long braided moustache gave him the look of wearing a menacing frown. Only the odd white lock amongst the nest of brown hair betrayed the passage of time.

"What's this?" he yelled, surveying the men armed and ready for trouble. "Knab, are you telling me I can't pay you a wee visit? Can you not see my shield hanging from the mast there?"

Knab stepped forward wearing a neutral expression on his face and replied, "Kindron, my sight's as good as it ever was."

Kindron strode right up to Knab. "Then stand your folk down or I'll have to hurt them," the Sea Wolf captain ordered, grinning up at Knab. When Knab gave no order to disperse, Kindron slapped his old comrade's arm and declared, "You're still as stubborn as ever."

"Some things don't change. If what I hear's true, you're still as big a bastard as ever."

Kindron's smile froze for an instant before his laughter rang through the fjord, forcing him to bend over and clutch his gut from the fits of it. He fooled no one with his forced hilarity and it was Knab's turn to wear a frozen smile. When he finally halted his laughter, Kindron said, "Come now Knab, take me into your mighty roundhouse there and let's talk over some of your ale. I don't need a fight, I've come for a tithe of *lifgyld*." His eyes fell on Cairn, Lars, and Thay then, and he added, "Those lads there look a bit green yet, but maybe ripe enough to pull an oar."

Knab turned his head and took in the youngsters, but he took full notice of Lora where Kindron seemed to have overlooked her. Worry was etched on her features and she clutched nervously at a leather thong that was strung around her neck. The Darnok chieftain said, "That one won't like her birthing day this winter."

"Ah yes," Kindron said as he finally noticed the auburn-haired young woman. He stared at the four adolescents and then continued, "It was these four babes and the rumours that ran along the fjords of them bringing good luck to the Darnok that led you to this squalid sheep outpost in the first place, wasn't it? You took it as a sign of Florri's blessing." Then he looked up again at Knab and asked, "Was it really so long ago? Rulla be fucked! Fifteen years gone by already."

"Don't go all teary-eyed, Kindron. That's why I wanted off your boats in the first place."

Kindron laughed again and tugged Knab towards the round-house. He beckoned his crews with his other arm and soon the whole village and the Sea Wolves were drinking together indoors. "I can't believe it!" Lars whispered to the three other youths as they made their way to the roundhouse. "I didn't think we'd see the Sea Wolves until the fall, or maybe even next spring. Think of it! - tonight we'll be in a different clan!"

"You'll be in a different clan," Lora shot back. The three boys all looked closely at her then and saw her sorrow. Tears welled up in her eyes and she ran off towards her home. The boys fell into a sombre mood as they watched her run.

§

Lora did not attend the beginning of the feast. She ordered her younger sister Nalane to stay in the roundhouse and keep an eye on Rutgar and Henkal before dragging her parents, Uilig and Loska, home to their kitchen table. She asked them to sit down and stood in front of them. She took a deep breath, but before she could begin, Uilig held up a hand and said, "I know what you would say, Lora, but the lads must leave. Rig and Renith served with the Sea Wolves, as did I, and they want their boys to go. If Leigh were here and not in his summer ranges, he'd be just as pleased ... why do you think he decided to leave Cairn here in the first place? It's time for them lads to become men by serving all Fjordlanders, putting our enemies on their heels and keeping the Horothian ships patrolling their own waters and not ours."

"Father, I know," Lora replied. "I know. It's just that I cannot bear to be separated from them. But I don't want them to stay either. I want to go with them." Loska gasped and Uilig's jaw dropped open. Before they could cobble together a response, she continued, "I have thought long on it, father, mother. The old seer, Helgya, sailed with the Sea Wolves when she was as old as I am. Mum, didn't you make one sailing beyond the Teeth? What Helgya saw and learnt made Krannogberg stronger. Mum learnt enough that she orders Krannogberg's defences for Knab. I would do the same; I would go to the Sea Beyond the Teeth and come back better for it."

Uilig stammered, "Lora, but ..." before turning to Loska

Loska stood and pulled Lora into a tight embrace. "Oh my Lora. I am proud of the fire that burns in you. Are you sure you want to do this? I have something of the seeress in myself and I know that it is a dangerous path that is laid in front of those boys."

"I am sure," Lora declared.

Uilig finally found his words, "Listen to your mother. Have you gone mad? Your place is here in Krannogberg, child."

Loska turned and slapped Uilig' head. "She's no child! She's sixteen and now a fully grown woman. I did not counsel her to stay, I asked her if she was sure of herself. She is, and I'm even prouder of her for it. She'll go with my blessing ... and a dagger or two hidden under her skirts to accompany Íss. She might just turn into our next Helgya, or follow in my footsteps."

Uilig's jaw dropped open again. Then he blurted out, "Don't listen to your mother! She's gone mad! Madder than you. You cannot go."

"Once she's declared her will, she cannot stay, Uilig."

"But ... on a vessel with Sea Wolves! You can imagine what could happen to her!"

"She's quicker than me when I went, and I was quick enough with a dagger to defend myself. And do you think those boys would ever allow anything to happen to her?"

"The boys won't be in command! And they'll be up against hardened Sea Wolves!"

Loska got to her feet. "Exactly. So you and I need to go speak to a few people. Come on, we've got to go before drunkenness robs them of their senses. Bring your purse."

Uilig gaped up at his wife and only managed another, "... but ..."

"Listen, Uilig my love, the whole village knows these four children have *wyrds* that are different from all others. For the boys, well, we all knew the Sea Wolves would pluck them from our village. But I have long wondered what path would present itself to Lora. I had wondered if Helgya's wayfaring in her youth, and my own, might not call to her. If Lora knows this to be her path, I would help set her on it." Then she narrowed her eyes into a menacing look, smiled and added, "And so would Kindron ..."

§

Uilig found Rig and Renith at the centre of the roundhouse, staring into the hearth and murmuring to each other while the revelling went on around them. Uilig pulled up a stool and sat between them. "You've spoken with your lads?" he asked.

"Aye" Rig replied. "We did indeed."``

"And Cairn?"

Renith nodded. "Leigh knew this would be the year. He spoke to me before he and Fallig left. I just gave the boy his father's battle axe, so he knows better now why Fallig wept on the day they left." Uilig nodded.

"How does it go with Lora," asked Rig.

Uilig glanced over his shoulder at Loska hovering nearby, following the conversation. Then he looked up into Rig's blue eyes and replied, "Strangely, if the truth be known. Listen, I need you to speak up for me with Kindron." Rig and Renith arched eyebrows in curiosity, but then looked at each other and nodded.

After the meal, but well before the time that most feasts would see their last keg of ale cracked open, Cairn, Lars, and Thay were brought forward by Knab, Renith, and Rig. The bard, Kyre, stopped his music and a hush fell over the round-house. Kindron stood up, crossed to the hearth and pulled a flaming brand from it. He turned to Knab and chanted:

Sea Wolf wrath is the fire that burns in your veins
and gives you life.
Sea Wolf strength holds strife from your shores.
Sea Wolf courage gives you power.
So as you take,
you shall give.
I demand lífgyld.

Knab pushed Cairn forward, Renith and Rig doing the same with their own sons, and the chief replied:

Take our sons   to other shores.
Turn leaf to stem.   Make them men.

Kindron turned to the crowd of the roundhouse and yelled:

Sea Wolves harken now   kin has come from kith,
bringing arms for oars   meet your new brothers
Cairn, Lars, and Thay!

His shout was greeted by a loud roar from all those present, Darnok and Sea Wolf alike.

"Is that it?" Thay asked in disbelief.

"In villages that don't cooperate so much as your Krannogberg, the initiation rite is a bit more robust!" Kindron stated with a grin. "More's the pity that your sheep-herding families want rid of you. We're your family now, younglings."

The night became one of drink and song. Kyre belted out the old sagas of his time among the Sea Wolves and his successor, a wiry blond man named Erig, sang of the trophies Kindron had garnered over the years since. Of course, two bards could never occupy the same roundhouse for a night of revelry without a duel breaking out. Kyre and Erig challenged themselves to a duet; the Saga of Iolanda and Rigar, one of the longest in Fjordlander lore, and certainly the one with the most complex harp work. The trick to the duel was that one could sing however many verses he liked before dropping the song into the lap of the other, who was expected to miss no more than a beat of rhythm. They got through the Meeting, the Courting, the Scorning, the Despairing, the Wayfaring of Rigar, the Sojourning of Iolanda, and the Reckoning before finally Erig dropped an extra half beat on the transition. He sang out the rest of that couplet, handed the tune to the winner, rose, and bowed to the veteran musician and poet, accepting his defeat. Kyre then finished off the saga to rousing approval.

Krannogberger and Sea Wolf alike danced to the jigs and sang of the children of ale, and if no new children of ale were conceived that night, it was not from want of trying. As Erig recounted the sacking of the grand city of the Moortok and the slaughter of its pathetic defenders even though they outnumbered the Fjordlanders four to one, even Kyre deigned to acknowledge to Kindron that he had found himself an "adequate" replacement on his boats for the best bard in Fjordland. The two bards later lifted jugs of ale together and cemented their bond by joining harps for a rousing version of the Saga of Lindstrum, the great Sea Wolf who tricked Asgear, Lord of the Waves, into a lifetime of safe passage through the Demon's Teeth in trade for a goat.

The next morning, with the Godspace above the fjord changing from its summertime golden-tinged navy of night to the gold of a sunny day, the villagers gathered to see off the Sea Wolves with their new clan members. The two bards were the last to present themselves; they shuffled from Kyre's cottage, blinking against the brightening day and holding their heads against what must have been fierce pounding coming from inside their skulls. The Sea Wolf warriors formed up in front of their boats and the boys stepped forward. They looked the part, decked out in their fathers' gear, for the most part, and with the face guards of their helmets hiding their youth almost as much as the height and bulk they had acquired. They each wore boiled leather armour - Cairn had been warned about wearing his father's mail on board and it was wrapped in an oil-sodden cloth in a sea chest that he held under his arm. Both Thay and Cairn had battle axes hooked into their belts, though Cairn also had *Orgor's Awl*, his big maul, hefted over his shoulder, while Lars had a well-sharpened and well-polished *Harbinger* hanging on his back. The claymore's rich, elaborately worked pommel protruding from Lars' scabbard caught the eye of many a Sea Wolf. Then Uilig stepped up and gently pushed Lora towards Kindron. "Here she is," he said. "Her mind's still set, so I pass her into your care. I expect you to be true to your word."

"Have no fear, fisherman. You've given me fair *bondgyld*. She's under my shield now." Kindron replied. "We'll pass her into the clan tonight."

"What's this?" asked a burly, black-haired man with his beard tied into a single braid upon his chest. He had a broad red scar beneath his right eye that made him look as if he leered at everyone upon which he cast his gaze. "A goodbye kiss for the captain?" Guffaws rippled around the man but Lora strode forward to join her three friends.

"Lora here will be sailing with us at the special request of her father," Kindron declared.

"This is a welcome first!" the scarred man exclaimed. "Now the clans give us their girls willingly. We'll share her around during the voyage!" His leering and laughter was suddenly cut off as Lars and Thay lunged at him, dragging him to the ground. Cairn bolted forward and kicked at the man's head before any of the Sea Wolves could come to the defence of their companion. Then the warrior clan surged forward in a mass. Only a half-dozen Sea Wolves could get in on the fight, but they peeled off Cairn, Thay, and Lars, tossing each one to three or four of their fellows who set in on the young men, benevolently sharing in the joyful free-for-all. Knab, Rig, Renith, and Uilig jumped in to help the youngsters, Knab striking Sea Wolves with the butt of his great axe, and the others flailing in the confusion with their fists. Kindron hollered, ordering his people back to their boats, but few chose to hear him over the din of the mêlée.

A sudden blast on a war horn brought a pause to the chaos. The Sea Wolves and the Darnok alike stood and looked to the fjord to see the danger. But the only danger was Loska, who stood at the edge of the men, the horn in one hand, a spear in the other, and a look on her face so stern it could peel the paint off Rena's newly-painted lintel. "If you children do not grow up right this instant, the women of this town will have to take a switch to each and every one of you!"

The combatants stared at her in silence until Kindron burst into laughter and leapt up onto the prow of his ship, *Rignil*. "Well said, woman! Into the boats, lads, or I'll flail you myself ... though perhaps I shouldn't deprive this good woman of the pleasure; she looks like someone who has a strong arm and a good memory for holding grudges!" Then he turned to the man who had insulted Lora and said, "Bjarni, that'll teach you to keep some manners about you when in the presence of women. Keep your black eyes to yourself, hear? That goes for you all. She's under my shield. Got it? She's part of our clan now. You've taken vows to defend each other; that now includes her."

Kindron caught some muttering from the mass of Sea Wolves and barked, "And that's enough griping about angering Florri! I don't know if women on a ship is bad luck or not; I've not the wisdom of Rulla. But old Magon, the Darnok's Priest of Hondrig, says She drew a special rune for this one. Lora here is touched; she might have the gift of the Sight, so think on that when you worry about a gale driving us onto some rocky shore!

"And if that isn't good enough for you, thanks to Lora's folks, we have a *bondgyld* we could use to stock up on ale before we head south, or wine once we're there! Think on whether having a woman along's not worth it on a stinking hot day as we lie off the Straelish coast pouring out cool draft from a keg of the best bitter from Toftig's Tower!"

While that did not set the crews cheering, it did cut out the grumbling. As the gruff man, Bjarni, stalked off to the furthest longboat, Lora swayed on her feet and whispered:

Bjarni will endure great suffering
  but after,
    there are horses as this land
    has never seen,
    riches and renown.

Kindron steadied Lora with a hand grasping her elbow and he exchanged a questioning glance with Loska. Lora's mother just smiled and said, "I told you."

With that, Kindron turned to the four new Sea Wolves and said, "You, girl, you sail with me at the stern of this boat. You," pointing at Cairn, "come aboard too. You'd capsize the smaller boats with the weight of you. *Rignil's* got draught enough for your likes. You," pointing at Lars, "take an oar with your friend and keep an eye on him. Aught comes to pass and I'll hold you responsible. You," pointing at Thay, "Toftig'll take you in the second boat over there."

"No," Thay said in a surprisingly calm voice given the new, little-known life upon which he was to embark. "I go with you in your boat."

A hush fell on the gathering. Kindron narrowed his eyes, glared at the youngster and said, "I will order the disposition of my ships as I see fit. You go with Toftig in *Thunderer*."

"Unless you see fit to order Rulla to your disposition, then I go with you in your boat."

"Why's that, sheep-herder?" Kindron asked, a frigid fire alight in his frosty blue eyes.

"She spoke to me," Thay replied, pointing to *Rignil's* mast.

A few of the Sea Wolves chuckled at that but Kindron hushed them up with a sharp glance. "What do you mean, she?"

"The dragon on your sail."

"You haven't seen my sail. We rowed into this fjord. There was no wind."

"I heard her nevertheless."

Kindron exploded with laughter and said, "Then your hearing's a damn sight better than mine, sheep-herder." Many Sea Wolves laughed at their leader's quip, but those closest to the captain held their breath until Kindron sighed deeply. Then the captain exchanged a knowing glance with old Magon, arched an eyebrow and said in his usual, loud voice, "Get in, then. You'll be sorry soon enough to have me as your captain. You can take care of that bear of a friend of yours then, and make sure he doesn't sink us all."

Chapter Two

For all his bluster, Kindron seemed to realize that Thay and Lars knew their way about a boat, so he assigned Thay and Cairn to one oar and put Lars on the oar behind them. Lars found himself in the company of a burly, scarred warrior named Krüllig Sohygar who looked nearly twice his twenty-four years and who sported a bushy blonde beard. Krüllig welcomed him to the ship with a grin and a wink, whispering, "I enjoyed your wee message to Bjarni. He's had it coming. He'll stew on it, and that vision of your friend's, for a while." A developing black eye kept Lars from winking back with his left eye - he never learnt how to wink with his right eye without contorting his face - but he nodded in appreciation. Knowing his oar mate was not going to try to pitch him overboard the first time he turned his back was a great relief to him. He also marvelled at how quickly the tale of Lora's vision had spread among the Sea Wolves.

Lars noted that Kindron put Lora by the tiller even though she could pull an oar just as well as anyone. Krüllig caught the direction of Lars' gaze, chuckled and said, "I'll wager her auburn hair has caught his eye and he's loathe to have her far from his side." Lars turned his gaze to Krüllig to see if the man was hinting at something indecent, but his oar mate winked again and added, "Don't worry, he takes good care of those under his eye. He'll look out for her."

Others among the crew noted where Lora sat, too, though they would have been surprised by the numerous questions Kindron posed to her. Indeed, Kindron seemed to understand rapidly that she was quick-witted and not shy of letting him know her point of view, captain and leader of the Sea Wolves or no. Lars heard her as she pointed out shallows and safe passages - though he suspected a captain like Kindron would know the Bight well. Even so, the chieftain quizzed Lora about the currents that swirled close to Hargur's Head, the shallows that might extend beyond the fjord's many points and spits, as well as the way the winds buffeted off the highlands. But Lars also thought back to something he had overheard the previous evening when Loska had bent close to Kindron at the feast and had said that Lora showed signs of the Sight. Lars suspected that Lora's mother may have convinced the Sea Wolf captain that Lora's developing talent might keep them off reefs, if not her knowledge of local currents and hazards.

As they slipped out of the Andersfjord and onto Hondrig's Bight, Lars felt a profound joy. He was finally setting out on the journey that he had always sought - a passage to manhood as much as to any foreign shore where the wealth of soft southerners would help his people. He smiled as he heaved on his oar beside the bushy-bearded blonde man. He glanced at the sea chest underneath his bench, to which he had lashed *Harbinger* in its oiled cloth, and his smile turned into a grin. A song rose unbidden to his lips and he belted it out. His fine voice flew upon the waves and by the second line, every hand on board had joined in:

Sires rowed thus before us,
    carving oars into the waves,
crashing down on foreign shores,
    storm winds filled their sails.
Southern curs cowered 'fore them,
    their pillage bought with blood.
Who stands agin' us breathes their last,
    the Sea Wolves never fail.

Rise now my brothers, rise to the wave!
    Take up the oar and rise to the wave!

We who now row after,
    our steel is just as sharp.
Driven on by elder tales,
    and the wicked northern gale,
who can hold their shores agin' us?
    Who refuse our price?
We shall never flounder,
    the Sea Wolves never fail.

Rise now my brothers, rise to the wave!
    Take up the oar and rise to the wave!

Should a brother taste his own blood,
    fall to a worthy foe,
or swim in the cold dark deep,
    close bright eyes behind the veil,
we'll fight with renewed vigour,
    and slay the lowly foe,
sing our brother's glories,
    the Sea Wolves never fail.

Rise now my brothers, rise to the wave!
    Take up the oar and rise to the wave!

§

Lars' elation - and that of the entire clan - lasted through the whole of the day and into the bright evening. Only two crew members seemed not to be enjoying themselves; Cairn, who had never spent much time on a boat and whose muscles were not used to the long, repetitive work of pulling the oar; and a captive named Yens from a land to the east who sat three benches ahead of them. Krüllig answered a query from Lars, "Him? He's a sullen man if there ever was one. That's why we always keep him in shackles." Then with a laugh he added, "Though maybe it's the other way around ... he's sullen because we keep him in shackles? That bears some thought! Ha, ha!"

That evening they put in at Sagear's Cove on Langsand Island. Krüllig told them that rather than expend their own stores of supplies, they would put in at towns and extract their tithe. If one of the other Sea Wolf clans had already done so, Krüllig told them that they would "usually" accept board, though occasionally would exact a further tithe if they thought their welcome too stingy or the host clan too wealthy. "Mind, we're a bit less pushy if the clan be well organized, like what Knab's done to you lot in Krannogberg." The Higgersuld clan had already paid its tithe, so after the ritual confrontation on the beach between the chieftain and Kindron, the Arctic Wolves were promised food, a barrel of ale, and the roundhouse for the night.

The youngsters learnt something of the Sea Wolves' routine then. Kindron drew staves from under *Rignil's* benches and threw them down onto the beach - as did the captains of the other longboats - so that each man could take one up. Thus they initiated the sparring. The time between putting in and sunset was dominated by combat practice. Kindron threw each of the three lads a wooden stave weighed at the far end with a length of iron and wrapped in cloth. Then he threw the lads to the wolves, or at least the Sea Wolves, as the rough, mock combat began. Kindron didn't know just what to do with Lora, so when she offered to join in to improve her shield work, he agreed with a laugh and fought her himself.

Lars loved it: men yelling and laughing, many wagering on the bouts of the new arrivals, all cheering on Lora in her battles against Kindron, the quick young woman proving hard to hit, though she never managed to strike the Sea Wolf captain. The locals rolled the promised barrel of ale down from the village, cracked it open and ladled out drinks to bare-chested brutes of Sea Wolves. Krüllig grabbed one of the younger, bigger Arctic Wolves by his shirt and thrust him at Lars, yelling, "Here's Stamma. He's shite with the sticks. You'll have a chance with him." And Lars did indeed have a chance. He landed five hits to Stamma's two. Then Krüllig himself took up the stave and only won four to three. He challenged anyone who teased him for being handsome, or who mocked not having earned his white-blonde braid of hair, landing hits unexpected of a raw recruit. Lars soon figured out that many Sea Wolves had trouble when he wielded his stave one-handed, as if it were *Harbinger* with an ability to dart in and jab instead of some imaginary axe, with broad sweeps and arcs. He managed to land a few jabs before anyone figured out when to leap back, roll aside, or simply strike at the stave being held in one hand rather than two and thus attempt to knock it from Lars' grasp.

After the bout with Krüllig, Lars' oar mate asked to see *Harbinger*. The new Sea Wolf fetched the claymore back from *Rignil's* deck and many warriors clambered around to look at it. "How did you hear about it?"

"Word's been a-spreading for a long time, my boy, with every new recruit from Krannogberg. This last spring, Dag Somorgin of the Black Wolves crowed about it being a *kunungr's* weapon, a king's blade, or some such thing."

They all gazed upon it with admiring eyes: even Kindron did not own so nice, or so storied, a weapon. Lars handed its pommel to his oar mate, who made a few swipes and jabs with it before handing it on to another Sea Wolf. Even Asgear Solief, *Rignil's* first officer, took time away from the sparring to look at the weapon. At length, Asgear handed it back and declared, "Well, though I doubt our folk'll accept a king, I'm glad that blade is on this voyage."

Back up the strand, Bjarni, the big, scarred, black-haired man with his beard tied into a single braid who had dared insult Lora, pointed at Cairn and yelled, "You! You spar with me!" The big man hauled off his woollen shirt and said, "So, your friend's seen suffering and riches for me, has she? We'll I can scry too! I can see into your future and I see suffering! No riches, mind, just suffering!" The older man's mood improved as he pummelled the young lad mercilessly, with Cairn getting more and more angry as he failed to block the blows. Finally the big young lad exploded in a fit of fury, spittle flying from his mouth as he flew into a whirling blur, the stave flailing and striking. Bjarni took a whack on the left biceps, a blow to the right leg and a final strike to his barrel chest before simply plucking the staff from Cairn's hands, casting it aside, and jumping on the youngster's back. Cairn bellowed in blind rage and bucked like a horse against the heavy mass pressing down on him. At length, laughing penetrated Cairn's consciousness. He found himself enclosed in a bear hug within a circle of merry onlookers, Bjarni laughing louder than the rest, but the laughter wasn't mocking - it was genuine mirth. Cairn looked over his shoulder at his adversary's face, seeing the hard eyes and the broad red scar blazing on his right cheek, but he saw wonder, not malice.

"Calm lad," the man said, loud enough for all to hear. "That'll do. Settle down." When he figured Cairn was listening, he relaxed his bear hug and proclaimed, pointing to the red welts on his arm and chest, "Would you look at these wee prizes! Lads, I say we've ourselves one of Karn's own berserkers like the days of old." Then to Cairn he added, "You get the movements of your axe mastered so that you need no thinking to control it, then when you give yourself to the Goddess of War like that again, you'll be the greatest warrior She's seen in a generation."

Cairn cast a stunned gaze around the circle of spectators. Finally a grin cracked his face and he said, "Karn's work builds a thirst." Then he called out, "Where's the ale?"

Bjarni grinned back and summoned another Sea Wolf to come forward with a ladle from the barrel. A roar of laughter rose as Cairn downed its contents in two swallows, threw it aside, snatched up *Orgor's Awl*, and swung it at Bjarni again, triggering another bout.

Never in his short life had he felt agony of throbbing bruises as he did that night trying to sleep in the roundhouse, and agony had never felt so sweet.

For his part, Thay discovered that even relative to hardened Sea Wolf warriors, hauling on oars and fishing nets had made him strong. His height gave him an edge in reach, though his skill required improvement, for while he could get in the odd hit, he found himself on the shingle beach far too often. And yet, something told him that how he swung an axe would matter less to him than the other Arctic Wolves, and he glanced over at Lars wielding the stave one-handed.

After the sun went down and the long summer twilight drew in, the sparring ceased and the youngsters learnt another element of their new routine, time spent with the captive, Yens. Once they stowed the staves away aboard the longboats, Kindron ordered that instead of singing to Erig's songs with the townsfolk, they spend their time with Yens after sparring each night so that the youngsters would learn something of the man's tongue, Straelish. This learning was the only taint to an otherwise perfect day for Lars as he didn't like the southern tongue and wanted to spend his time ashore singing and getting to know the members of his new clan. Cairn, too, would have preferred spending his time ashore getting to know a barrel of ale in addition to the singing, but he accepted his fate without complaining. Unlike Lora and Thay, neither of the two of them had ever spent much time with Aganas, the Straeling wife of Gunder Sohargar back home, so the learning was difficult for them. In contrast, Lora and Thay enjoyed that time, proof as it was of their grand new adventure, one in which their small skill in the tongue already seemed to hold value.

Yens, for his part, spoke of his homeland, how the Straelings obeyed the holy word of their god, Galivith, and how his folk would be the instrument of Galivith's divine wrath against the evil that crashed against Straeland's shores. And, after the lessons had concluded, he glowered at the youngsters.

§

Sagear's Cove sent them on their way the next morning with a fresh cask of ale, though the crews would have preferred a barrel, and some of the less-diplomatic oarsmen grumbled that they should have searched the town until they had un-earthed two barrels. But Kindron ordered them into the ships and south they sailed.

That day they sailed past the near ghost town of Jorrums-fjord, where once the Jarlags had come ashore ravaging the Darnok's close kin, the Darnalths. Kindron bade the rowers rest and he summoned the four youngsters to him at the stern. He handed the tiller over to his first officer, Asgear, a gruff, burly man with clear blue eyes, shoulder length blonde hair, and long moustaches that draped down in two long braids over his bushy beard and past his chin. Kindron pointed to the poor, meagre collection of ramshackle huts and said, "There be Jorrumsfjord. Take a good long look. That sight tells me two things that I reckon you should know."

Of course it was Lora who couldn't wait, "What two things?"

Kindron smirked and held up a long finger, "Thing one; you should know I know you were Darnok. But you should remember that you're now in a family of a different clan, the Arctic Wolves family of the Sea Wolves clan. You've got my permission to look at that sight and feel rage after you pay me your *lifgyld* and decide you're Darnok again. Until that time, you're Sea Wolves, got it? Jorrumsfjord doesn't affect you.

"Thing two," he continued, holding up a second finger, "tomorrow night we put in at Sangspit and I need not tell you that's where the Jarlags call home. There'll be no trouble from you, because you're Arctic Wolves. And if anyone joins us from there and you cause trouble, you'll be causing trouble for an Arctic Wolf, not a Jarlag, got it?"

They nodded in reply, though each one of them found it difficult to do so.

Kindron put in at Jorrumsfjord, though only the captains of the three longboats, their first officers, their Priest of Hondrig, and Erig the Bard were allowed off the vessels. The Sea Wolf clan's leadership didn't stay long, they chatted for a while with the hamlet's elders, astonishingly giving over the cask of ale they had been given that very morning, before setting out again. The crew remained grim during the visit and not a single one voiced a complaint about the captains' openhandedness, though Thay - ever watchful and always pondering - noticed a good few who furrowed their brows and shook their heads on the outward voyage when the captains were not looking.

That night they put in at Spearberg, a much bigger town and home to the Farloag clan. Thay's father, Rig, had grown up in Spearberg, and he was happy to see the place again as they rowed up to the rocky strand. The nightly routine continued with the sparring, followed by the mangling of Straelish under Yens' tutelage, to the sounds of singing and celebration wafting aboard from dry land, but after that Thay and the others were allowed to go ashore, partake of the fun, and meet Thay's kin. His father had only taken him to visit twice before and he proudly showed off his friends to his uncles Gils and Odkel Sowulf as well as to the many cousins that they met. To their astonishment, most folk had heard of them as well as "our own Thay"; the tale of four bairns born of different mothers on the same storm-wracked night had evidently made its way up and down Fjordland's coast.

When it came time to pull the oars the next morning, the four of them suffered under the bright sun from an excess of Fjordlander hospitality the night before. Erig sat at the stern of *Rignil* that day and strummed an ode to throbbing heads for them. It must have been a well-sung song, for the crew soon took up the refrain - oh so loudly! - and at the end slapped them on their backs. And of course, Lora, Lars, and Cairn all blamed Thay for their misery. It was awful.

Spearberg sat just up the coast from Caljürd's Arm, the protected waters of the Jarlags. That very day, *Rignil, Thunderer,* and *Northern Fire* skirted the shoals at the arm's entrance, crossed over the reefs at high tide, and hauled themselves through the rampant currents where the arm met the sea. All the while they were watched by the crew of a longboat. The Arctic Wolf captains had hung their shields on their masts, so the longboat hove to instead of attacking them, and escorted them into the calm waters of Caljürd's Arm. The fjord was impressive, long and narrow with steep walls that rose high up onto the plateau above. It ran roughly straight from its western mouth, so it afforded good views of the Boldring Mountains to the east.

They soon caught sight of Sangspit at the eastern extremity of the arm and as they approached, Lars had to admit that the town was as at least as proud as Krannogberg. Although the Jarlags hadn't built a curtain wall around the settlement like his home, it had many more houses. Its roundhouse was very tall and well-adorned, with the ends of the wooden beams that supported the roof carved into representations of the Gods. There were trading houses, smoke houses, a bakery, all things that Lars had never before seen but of which he had only heard tell in Kyre's stories. And there were a lot of people, far more than in Krannogberg, busy mending ropes, gutting fish, shifting barrels, hammering together cottages, repairing shingles on roofs, parents running after toddlers, or toddlers running away from parents ... the things of a normal life and hardly the conduct of ravening monsters, as all the tales he had ever heard contended. And yet, Lars knew that these were the Darnok's bitterest rivals, a clan willing to enslave or kill his folk … his former folk. He shook his head; his new life would take some getting used to.

They sailed past the town to put in on the pebble beach that lay just beyond. Instead of a show of force, the Sea Wolves were met on the beach by a lean, solitary man, covered in scars and with dark hair streaked by grey. Lars remembered him from the Battle of Krannogberg those few years before. Rigald Sokaroth, the crafty Jarlag chieftain, met them, alone on the strand. He already had three barrels of salted beef and a half-dozen sacks of grain beside him. He also had a claymore, as beautiful - and as rare - as *Harbinger*, in his hands, point sticking down into the beach's pebbles. As *Rignil* ground to a landing, settling on those pebbles with a crackling crunch as a heavy wave recoiled back into the dark sea, Sokaroth nodded to Kindron swinging down from the prow and called out, "You're late."

"I do not come and go at your beckoning, Rigald," Kindron called back with a smile.

Sokaroth did not smile back, "We've got your tithe."

"You'd be insulted if I replied, 'You'd better have,' wouldn't you?"

"I reckon you're right," Sokaroth agreed, nodding.

"This is the year. I've got them," Kindron declared.

"Is it? Where are they?"

"On board *Rignil*. They're Sea Wolves now. If anything were to befall them, I would make it my life's purpose to make sure it went ill with the Jarlags."

"They'd best stay off shore. I can control my hatred, but others here might not."

Kindron smiled at that. "Perhaps not. Though let me put it this way, if anyone's hatred touches these vessels or those upon them, you'd best take your clan and flee for the mountains."

"It'll be easier if they stay onboard, I'll say that. Though I'll say one more thing. Any Sea Wolf vengeance here for touching vessels would have to be visited upon us by another Sea Wolf clan, for none of your kind would be left alive. I think we understand each other."

"We do," Kindron replied.

That night Erig didn't sing many songs and the crews danced no jigs. For their part, the four youngsters didn't spar. They did stay onboard the vessels, with guards set upon them, and they did learn a lot of Straelish swear words they realized Aganas had never taught to Lora and Thay. Though he had little interest in remembering common Straelish words, Lars had a good ear for mischief and soon mastered, "perfidious puke breath!", "devil spawn", "Sheaf of Galivith!"

"What's Straelish for '*føukke*'?" Cairn asked.

"'*Føukke*'?" Yens echoed. "I have heard it much among your folk. It is not a simple curse, like 'damned' ?"

"It means 'copulate'," Lora clarified.

"Ah!" Yens responded. "That's why you use it so much." He glared at the youngsters, glanced down at his chains, and explained, "In my tongue it is '*foxt*', though it should never, ever be used." Cairn's eyes gleamed with glee.

"What about '*schijtte*'?" Thay asked, leaning in closer.

"Like 'dung'?" Yens shrugged. "That's just '*skeetze*'. You can even use that in polite company, such as an audience with your *herg*?"

"'*Herg*' ? That's like 'jarl', no? A lord?" Lora interjected.

Yens nodded. "We use *skeetze* all the time."

In the time it takes for lightning to crack the sky, Thay and Cairn soon had developed a standard dialogue; in their novice's accents, one would say "*foxt!*" and the other would respond with "*skeetze!*" or vice versa, repeated infinitely.

Lora, though, thinking back to time spent with Aganas, thought the words sounded awfully similar to the Straelish words for "nostril" and "twig".

§

They sailed out the next morning with two new recruits, a spindly, nervous lad of perhaps fourteen called Argus, and a massive brute of a youth named Jörgen. Kindron split them up and put them aboard *Thunderer* and *Northern Fire*. As the chieftain clambered aboard, he gave the Krannogberger youths a long, measuring look, though he did not reiterate his warning to think of themselves as Sea Wolves henceforth. The mood of the crews rose high as they left Caljürd's Arm under a brilliant azure sky.

Cairn's spirits were as high as anyone else's that morning, even though he had never held as romantic a vision of becoming a Sea Wolf as Lars. While he had never expected sloth and luxury, he had nevertheless looked forward to becoming an adult and making his own way in the world. He had always envisaged himself, axe in hand, overcoming inferior men and impressing foreign beauties in the doing. However, time onboard quickly removed from Cairn any romance he might ever have harboured regarding life among the Sea Wolves. Although sparring occurred every night, he used an axe more often to chop firewood for the nightly stays on damp, rocky, wind-swept beaches. He was ill-practiced at the work aboard ship and, to his shame, other oar mates would often have to re-do tasks that Kindron or Asgear had assigned to him, be it reefing the sail, tying down a line or battening down a tarp to keep pouring rain from drenching them. When the wind died and the crew rowed, he could feel through the oar he pulled with Thay that his friend struggled to make sure they maintained the right rhythm. Thay also took the lead in breaking out and stowing the oar when Asgear barked out the order. His took only small solace from Asgear recognizing his skill in smelting iron, giving him work during evenings ashore helping make or repair nails and other tools.

Worst of all, Cairn learnt to his harrowing embarrassment that shitting over the gunnel in high seas took greater coordination than he would ever have imagined or had yet mustered. He had to resort to the use of a bucket, and, the squat and toss method. He wouldn't have minded quite so much about the squat and toss if Lora hadn't gone and shown off immediately after his first, disastrous, sopping attempt at relieving himself. In contrast to his failed efforts, she braved the terrifying swells, whipped down her breeches and balanced herself expertly on the rail. Unlike Cairn, though, she had to brave catcalls, to which she responded by cracking a sarcastic smile and ordering Asgear, Kindron's first officer - ordering, no less! - to bring her the helmet of the loudest of the catcalling men. The grizzled Sea Wolf's clear blue eyes sparkled and the smile that came to his face sent his long, braided moustaches wiggling. He scooped up Snorri Sosnorri's helm and tossed it to her. Perched there on the rail, pitching up and down, she snatched the heavy object out of the air one-handed. Then she held it beneath her.

Snorri surged to his feet but a grinning Asgear pushed him back down onto the bench, the sparkle in his eyes replaced with menace. Lora finished her business, hopped back off the rail and, as she readjusted her breeches with one hand, she tossed the helmet onto Snorri's lap with the other, diverting eyes off her crotch while drawing them to Snorri's. The helm dripped into an expanding damp spot on the Sea Wolf's tunic, who looked down at it and then back up to Lora. She assumed her place next to Kindron, a coy smile on her face, and exclaimed, "You didn't think I'd just … ? No! I just wanted a wee rinse. It's sea water."

The crew burst out laughing, mirth in which even Snorri finally joined. A little later Lora took the helm back off Snorri and spent the rest of the afternoon polishing and oiling it for him, saying, "I've sailed on the Bight enough to know what salt water can do to good iron." That night on the strand he strutted around showing off his gleaming piece of armour and crowing about how it had never looked so good.

After that first incident, the only person to suffer catcalls on *Rignil* as he shat was Cairn.

That night when they were anchored off the town of Karn-hagen on the southern part of the island of Struno, after their lessons in Straelish, Cairn asked Lora about her brashness. "What got into your head, ordering Asgear about as though you were the first officer, not him? And wasn't that a dangerous game you played with Snorri?"

Lora shook her head and huffed.

"What?" Cairn asked, a note of confusion creeping into his voice. "Is the question so daft as all that?"

"Aye, it is," Lora retorted.

Cairn noted Thay and Lars glance questioningly at each other, reflecting his own puzzlement. "Well?"

Lora shook her head again and responded, "Sure, how'd I have ever managed to tolerate you three oafs since the day I was birthed if I didn't know how to turn the witless idiocy of young boys on its head?"

Cairn frowned. "Snorri's no young boy," he declared.

"Is that so? At that moment, you could have fooled me." The boys swapped shrugs and perplexed looks. At length, Lora sighed and explained, "Look, you three are my closest friends, but you're all boys, males. What do you suppose happens when some bastard gets it into his head that a girl needs putting in her place and there's no one around to know better? I'll tell you what happens, the girl had better be able to knock sense into the bastard, herself, or make sure she's never, ever, alone with him. The thing is, those bastards are usually better at knocking people about than the girl and it's hard to be under Kindron's shield every moment of the day. So, sometimes it's best to avoid drawing the ire of the bastards, getting them to like you, and at the same time reminding them who your friends are. Snorri now quite likes me. And everyone else now knows to steer clear of me or risk something more dire than you three coming after him; they'll have to deal with Asgear and Kindron, and likely Snorri as well."

"But how did you know Kindron wouldn't put a stop to you, you ordering his first officer around? How did you know Asgear would do what you ordered?"

Lora shrugged at that. "I just did. I'm getting these glimpses more and more now. A bit like Thay's crimson dreams, perhaps. I sense something with Asgear; something long, enduring, twisted, but close. My guess that he'd play along was good, I suppose. As for Kindron, my parents gave him *bondgyld* and I think that if my glimpses develop into something stronger, then he'll want me with him, not agin him."

Lars and Cairn nodded, still not fully understanding, but ready to accept the mystery. "It's all not fair," Thay finally stated.

"No, it isn't. Will you change it?" Lora asked, eyes looking to Thay as if searching his future.

Chapter Three

Lora's grim mood perhaps infected the Sea Wolves and their spirits dipped over the next few days as they neared the Demon's Teeth, a long mountainous archipelago that jutted from the mainland and marked the southern extent of Fjordlander settlement. The islands were an extension of the Boldring Mountains that joined the sea at Cape Terror. Every Fjordlander knew that the jagged islands derived their name from the way that they rose from the sea in sheer cliffs, and from the evil currents that swirled between them. When Lora prodded the crewmen to describe the Teeth, they shook their heads and replied, "You'll see for yourself soon enough."

Fjordlanders viewed the Demon's Teeth as a place of fear. The four youngsters had heard Kyre the bard sing of the dangers that a ship could face in the perilous passage through the many jutting peaks of the Teeth. One particular song sprang to Thay's mind as they approached the looming snow-capped islands. Unlike Lars, he did not have a mind for remembering hundreds of lines of verse but he remembered a few:

> *Dark fangs of rock came at us,*
> *the sea it heaved in swirls,*
> *the oars they snapped upon the cliffs,*
> *and men went overboard.*
> *The mountains moved, the narrows closed,*
> *no one true course exists.*
> *Your plunder is a bright fine thing,*
> *but it is a killing prize.*

The fleet came ashore at Toftig's Tower. At the end of a broad, arching, stony beach that was home to a colony of braying sea lions and flocks of shrieking sea gulls, it was the last safe place to come ashore before the Teeth. The tower made for a stark sight; a narrow, round construction made of rough hewn stones with a conical, shingled roof. Hard behind it stood the southernmost of the Boldring Mountains, rising up out of the green pine forests that enrobed them. A cluster of cottages surrounded the tower and Thay was surprised to see straw covering their roofs rather than shingles or turf. The tower kept watch on the Piligitswater and it was home to a Priest of Rulla, the Dealer of Fates, and a Priestess of Asgear, God of the Waves.

Krüllig had informed the youngsters that the resident priest would beg Rulla to select a fortunate rune for their sailing while the priestess would pray to Asgear for the safe passage of the Sea Wolves through the deadly waters of the Demon's Teeth. Every outgoing Sea Wolf expedition landed at Toftig's Tower to seek these necessary blessings, while every incoming one gave offerings in thanks for a safe sailing.

As they neared shore, heaving on their oars at the very end of a long day's rowing, Thay could not see the rising Demon's Teeth as he plied the oars, facing astern, looking out over the broad Piligitswater and its tall swells that slid in from the open ocean, but he could see the line of the Boldring Mountains stretching away to his right as they marched north towards his home. The mountains got him thinking of the place where the fleet was headed and he asked, "Who was Toftig? Is the captain of *Thunderer* named after him? Why is it called Toftig's Tower if it's a site of Rulla or Asgear?"

Cairn struggled beside him in agony - his hands were blistered and his muscles were still unused to the strain of rowing for long periods - and he could do no more than grunt his displeasure, but Lars replied from behind him, "Don't play the fool, Thay. You know right well." Thay heard Krüllig, Lars' oar mate, chuckle at the rebuke.

"I don't!" Thay protested. "Not everyone is an all-knowing bard like you, you ass."

"Sure, it's named for Rulla's warrior-priest who went with Mattic the Brave. And yes, of course *Thunderer's* captain's named for him. Have you not heard Kyre sing:

Rulla smiled upon him,
he who swung the axe,
trekking overland,
he who bowed in prayer,
Out of all his shipmates,
only he returned,
he who rode the wave,
he who bowed in prayer.
Toftig loved his shipmates,
the sea-road cast him here,
he built a place to watch
and pray for their return.

"Aye, I've heard the tune," Thay grumbled, "but I didn't know it was more than a tale."

"Ach, you'd best learn a bit of your history, hadn't you?"

"Right, then, he-who-only-knows-anything-if-its-in-a-song, why'd only he return?"

"I do too know things not in songs!" Lars huffed. Then he deigned to continue, " 'Cause only he survived the ... ow!" Lars grunted in pain as Krüllig elbowed him in the ribs. "What did you do that for?"

"Before we're there, you'd best not talk about what can happen in the Teeth, both of you, or what we want to occur there. You'll hex the sailing."

Thay kept his peace after that, but as they hauled *Rignil* up on shore in front of the watchtower, he finally cast his eyes at the Teeth, the towering line of mountains rising out of the water to the south. Tall and stone grey, they rose to snow-capped peaks. Indeed, their sheer faces gave them the look of fangs and Thay felt a shiver slither up his spine.

That evening, with the sun descending into the wide waters of the western ocean in a blaze of glowing orange refracting on the water and on the snow-capped mountains, Thay and the other Sea Wolves prayed in place of the usual sparring sessions. As was the tradition of the Sea Wolves, their own Priest of Hondrig, Niers Sodjernen, knelt with the crews, passing the responsibility of seeking the blessings of the Gods to the resident priest and priestess of the tower. The old man in Rulla's garb - a long black robe trimmed with red at the sleeves and collar - unsettled Thay for some reason he could not identify. The priest's grizzled grey beard mostly hid a wrinkled and scarred face, and his eerie blue eyes had a far-off look to them.

The priest led them through a sombre service, asking Florri, the God of Good Fortune, to be gracious in bestowing good luck on this latest Sea Wolf mission. He begged Guliveg to protect and shield them through the perils of rough seas and pointed swords to bring them back home safely. He then implored Norrgi for good winds and fair skies. Finally, he prayed to Rulla to bestow Her blessing on them. Once complete, the Priestess of Asgear held an earthen jug of sea water and a piece of driftwood above her head, then set them down on the beach before leading them in the *Rite of Wayfaring.* The rhythmic chant, with the emphasis on every seventh line, hypnotized the crew as she rocked back and forth. The rocking spilled the sea water onto the piece of driftwood at her feet. When she finished her chant she upended the jug, spilling the remnants of the water onto the driftwood. Then she smiled. "Yours is a historic sailing," she declared and the men cheered.

That night, as the more hardy Sea Wolves - led by Bjarni - took advantage of an evening safe on shore to drink and gamble deep into the night, Thay kept to the company of his friends after their learning with Yens. While they laughed together - Cairn the most loudly of them all - talking about their future, Thay could not get the priest's last chant from his head:

Their way is dangerous,
  but their hearts are true,
Protect them now,
  and guide them to their wyrds.

§

When they cast off from Toftig's Tower the next morning in the dark of the pre-dawn, no one sang any Fjordlander anthems. A grim silence lay upon the boats, broken only by the sound of oars plying the water and waves sloshing off the prow. The crews sent private prayers to Norrgi for good weather. South they went, at first, and then, as the sky turned grey around them, east, as they rounded Cape Terror.

Once they rowed past that jutting dagger of land, the seas grew wilder. *Rignil* went first, followed by *Thunderer* and then *Northern Fire*. The chop came at them from the east and from the south as well, jostling the crews. Cairn, trying to keep his balance on the bench beside Thay, gasped, "What's with the waves? They only go in one direction back home!"

Behind them, Krüllig chuckled and replied, "This is no lake like your Tallogswater, lad. Out here, waves can come back off a cliff face with near as much force as it had rolling in from the ocean! Thank Guliveg the chop's coming off only one cliff." Thay didn't take much succour from the veteran Sea Wolf's words.

As they sailed on from Cape Terror, the dawn showed that the mainland to the rowers' right - off *Rignil's* port gunnel - rose in sheer cliffs and the first of the Demon's Teeth neared on their left, off the ship's starboard beam. As if on cue, the winds found them; between mainland cliff and sea-bound tooth, the gusts buffeted the craft from changing directions.

Astern, Thay saw that Kindron had noticed the look of apprehension on Lora's face and the captain laughed, yelling, "Ach well, 'tis a dark day, with heavy, dark clouds, swirling winds and choppy seas. Put your backs into work, lads, the faster we go, the quicker we're through." He ordered the crew to furl the sail and Thay watched the image of the crimson dragon roll up. For some reason this saddened him.

Then the rain began. At first it was but a mist, hard to differentiate from the spray thrown at them by the swirling winds from the wash rising off the prow or from waves surging against their sides. It turned into a steady drizzle, though, a while later. Then, not long before midday, the drizzle turned to rain. "Wonderful," Lars muttered. "Can this get any worse?"

Before either Thay or Cairn could reply, Krüllig laughed and said with a wink to Lars, "Of course it could, lad! You should be glad this is a summer crossing. In winter, you could be treading freezing cold water and watching our stern slip beneath the waves! But I wouldn't worry too much about that; Kindron's been through the Teeth two-score times. He'll see us through."

As if to underline their captain's skill, Kindron delivered them a small blessing. He leaned against the rudder and turned them to port into a channel that ran east to west between two jutting islands. He brought *Rignil* close to the southern island's cliff face - perilously so, thought Cairn - and ordered oars raised. The crew all leaned forward on their oars, panting in the pouring rain, but laughing as well as they saw that Kindron had found a current that pushed them along faster than any wind could. Then only he had to work as he controlled the rudder, pushing it or heaving against it as need be. But he grinned as he did so and that grin gave them all a fire in their bellies to combat the cold rain. *Thunderer* and *Northern Fire* hove to, and they could hear their fellow Sea Wolves bellow their approval from the other boats.

Their respite lasted long enough for them to break out the rations and gobble down a damp meal. Kindron even threw down a skin full of wine for the crew to pass around - though the captain was careful not to allow anyone more than a single swig of the extremely rare liquid. "Bought with our Lora's *bondgyld*, that is!" he reminded his crew, ever looking to crush whatever superstition might linger about having a woman on the sailing, Thay guessed. Kindron's face, however, darkened at a low drumming of thunder that suddenly rumbled across the waves. Before it echoed off the cliffs, the men were back on the oars. By the time the boats shot out the other end of the channel, lightning arced between the Teeth. The clouds turned jet and sank lower to the water. The seas, too, surged and dipped, currents colliding and waves coming at them from every direction, once combining to heave the stern aloft and throw men backwards onto the oars of their crewmate.

Thay looked about him; he could not see Lars rowing behind him, but Lora, huddling near the stern, looked as worried as Thay felt. Beside him, terror was carved on Cairn's burly features: the big youth looked horrible, with his dark hair lank, wet, and clinging to his ashen face, his brown eyes red-rimmed and wide, and his head twisting from side to side as he shot panicked looks at the sheer cliffs bursting from the swirling sea on either side of their longboat. Thay felt Cairn strain against the oar, quickening the rhythm but for the countering control that Thay exerted; it would not impress the captain if they broke the unison of the crew. It occurred to Thay that though Cairn, the son of herders, had occasionally been on boats in the Andersfjord, his friend had never before sailed in a storm.

"Calm down," Thay grunted between oar strokes. "This crew looks like they know what they're about."

"They move!" Cairn hissed in his ear, loud enough to be heard over the howling wind but not so loud as their crew mates could hear.

"What?"

"The cliffs!" Cairn blurted out. "They close in on us!"

"You've listened to too many of Kyre's tales, that's just the boat shifting in the swirls," Thay responded, but he glanced at the mountains involuntarily as he did so. At first glance, it did indeed look like the great wall to starboard loomed closer and the cliff to port filled more and more of the roiling grey-black sky.

Suddenly thunder boomed overhead and echoed off the precipices around them. The deafening crash drowned the drumming of Asgear and wiped the grin of defiance off Kindron's face. Thay quickly realized how much he had drawn confidence from the captain. Kindron studied the low, swift-flying clouds and then ordered the sail unfurled and trimmed. *Rignil* listed away from the wind and Kindron braced himself against the tiller, keeping a course that Thay hoped would steer them clear of the huge fangs of rock that rose from the waves. Salt spray carried on the wind from the bow showered him and mingled with his sweat. Behind *Rignil*, Thay could see that first Toftig on *Thunderer*, and then Albig on *Northern Fire*, followed Kindron's example one after the other, unfurling and setting their own sails. He could see less to starboard as the boat leaned in the water, but he saw frothing whirlpools and white foam splashing off the ever-approaching cliffs to port. He gave a start when he heard the crash of a wave against a jutting point of rock not more than an oar's length from the gunnel.

They passed a headland to the south of them only to hear Kindron yell from the stern, "Hang on!" As Thay hooked his legs around the prop of the bench in front of him, he saw terror on Lora's face. Then the instant was gone as a wall of water hit them from starboard. As he rose into the air, he reached for the gunnel. He saw Cairn pitch sideways and flail at the bench. Then Thay flew.

When he broke the surface, he gasped from the shock of the cold water and fought to keep his head above the waves. Against the looming backdrop of the Tooth to the north of them, he saw the flotsam of the boat all around him; men, oars, cloaks, planking, sea-chests and rope bobbed on the water. Six men had gotten their bearings after having been thrown even further and they began swimming towards him, two clutching sea-chests for buoyancy and flutter-kicking. He twisted his head around and saw the boat floating low in the water only an oar's length from him; he had evidently hung on better than most. Improbably, the only person still in the boat was Cairn, though the slave, Yens, flailed in the water right next to the hull, attached by his chain to an oar lock.

"Thay!" Cairn yelled. "Grab onto the oar!" The big lad stood unsteadily and ran out an oar to his friend.

Thay swam to the oar, his arms and legs flailing as quickly as he could make them, but he had the presence of mind to call out, "Sit down, you ass! And lean to the other side of the boat!" Cairn did so, scrambling to a bench and then straining with his great strength to haul Thay to the gunnel. Thay scrambled over and helped Yens from the water as Cairn ran out his oar to the six men swimming closer.

As Thay pulled Yens into the boat, *Rignil* rocked again, hit by another wave, though smaller this time. He let Yens take up an oar and he sloshed over to the rudder. The wave that had tossed them overboard had also left the sail flapping in the wind, but pulling on the rudder only brought the water-logged boat around slowly. Thay looked then to the sea and saw another massive wave bearing down on them. Two swells would wash under them before it hit, but he knew the rudder would not turn the boat around quick enough to point the prow into the wave. By now only three other men were in the boat, counting Cairn, and they were not even seated at oars yet; Thay knew three could never pull a boat sitting so low in the water around in time.

Quick as he could, he pulled on the rope lashing the anchor to the stern, expecting the slip knot to give and release the heavy stone in its wooden cradle. The rope, however, was thick and sodden, and some misfortune had pulled the ends of the knot too tight to allow the loop to slip. As the first swell lifted the boat under him, he had to fix his legs and give the lashing a great heave. Still the knot would not give. He felt the boat jostle as the others pulled another man from the seas. He whipped out his dagger, pried its point into the knot and used the blade as leverage, hoping to loosen it. He glanced over and saw that it was not another man at all that had clambered into the boat, but Lora. He did not breathe a sigh of relief. Rather, he glanced at the approaching wave, suddenly much nearer, and put his entire strength behind a last heave of the rope. It gave way in a sudden rush and he fell back onto the deck, the anchor thumping onto the deck at the stern.

"Lora!" he yelled, throwing himself against the rudder again as the second swell passed under them. "Trim the sail!" She did not bother to reply but scrambled over to the loose ropes that set the sail. Thay lifted the anchor from the deck and heaved it astern, towards the rock face of the nearby Tooth rearing up from the frothing water. He could not heave it far, but he hoped it would be enough as it trailed its rope behind it, just as he hoped the water would be shallow enough for his gambit to work. As the anchor's rope unwound with a whir, the prow crept to starboard, towards the wave that approached with alarming speed.

Thay had time to remark that the cliffs to port - he thought them so close not so long ago - might drop too deep under the water for the anchor to bite. But then suddenly the rope stopped unwinding. He knew he had to change dramatically the angle of the prow to the wave and that pulling on the rope from the stern would have no effect. So, with the black wall of water looming above them, Thay grabbed hold of the slack coils of rope attached to the anchor and ran, bounding from bench to bench above the water in the boat, to the prow yelling, "Hang on." He looped the rope once over the prow, forming a noose for the wolf that was the figurehead, and he hung on for dear life. They were not going to make it, Thay suddenly realized in the moments before the wave hit. They did not have enough forward momentum to swing the boat around.

That was the moment that Lora got the sail properly trimmed. Being the daughter of a fisherman and so bold as to insist on accompanying her father out to sea to learn the handling of boats, she knew how to catch the wind in a sail. In the near-gale now blowing, she pulled the sail into position, it caught the wind and the boat lumbered forward. "Keep it trimmed as it comes about!" Thay yelled over the rumbling thunder.

And it did come about. As the sea welled up and the wave towered over *Rignil*, Lora kept the sail in the wind and they turned. Thay pulled on the anchor rope with all his might, tugging the prow southwards. The wave crashed against their starboard side at an angle, but the prow had come about enough to cut into the onslaught. The boat lurched but did not capsize or toss them overboard, and then the wave was past them.

Thay scrambled back to the rudder while Lora furled the sail and Cairn again ran out an oar to the men in the water. Only one other such wave hit them, but by then a sodden and swearing Kindron had relieved Thay at the rudder and had pointed the prow directly into the swell. The men hauled out of the sea had also bailed a great deal of water out of the boat and *Rignil* rode the waves with greater ease. "Well lads," Kindron bellowed as they laboured, "did you see that bit of sailing by our Lora there? I think we can safely say that this woman brings us good luck, not bad."

Lora paid Kindron no heed and instead looked about her. She called out, "Cairn, have you seen Lars?" Her big friend shook his head and joined her and Thay in searching the water around the boat for his friend's fair hair. Their worry, however, was short-lived; *Northern Fire* drew up beside *Rig-*

nil after having scooped up Lars, Bjarni and Krüllig. *Thunderer* lashed to their other side - the three boats now rafting together - and Toftig returned to them another five soaking wet crewmen - shivering, but all grinning. Kindron himself did the head count, and then repeated it with Asgear, before dousing the momentary elation. "Hossig's gone," he said simply. He strode from *Northern Fire's* port side to *Thunderer's* starboard side, looking into the dark water, the other two captains looking ahead and astern, but they saw nothing. "We'll mourn on the other side of the Teeth," he declared and then set about putting his boat in order.

The wind and seas had calmed enough that Kindron passed around his wineskin again and had his crew take a bite to eat. Then he had them finish the bailing, return the sea-chests to their owners and re-stow them, secure the rigging and order the sail. He took his own woollen blanket from beneath the deck and, though it was sodden, just like everything else, he draped it over Lora's shoulders, patting her on the back. He gave Thay and Cairn each a serious nod. All three knew they had just received Kindron's deepest thanks.

Finally the lashings between the boats were ordered undone, the anchor hauled up and the fleet took sail again.

§

Kindron pushed them hard on the oars after their near-disaster, and there were other moments when Cairn was sure they would be dashed against the cliffs, but they managed to clear the Teeth before nightfall. Cairn knew little about boats, but he could hear grunts of approval from Thay and Lars as Kindron guided them from one current to another between the Teeth. Towards the end of the afternoon, the winds blew more consistently from the west and they lost less time trimming the sails. The worst of the storm had passed them by, as well, with the thunder and lightning lumbering off east, ahead of them. As they cleared the last strait and Kindron let them stow their oars long enough to look beyond the prow at the open sea ahead of the ship, even the rain let up.

They dropped anchor in a small but well-sheltered cove at twilight. Kindron ordered campfires built on the narrow strand before the shallow cliffs, knowing that the work of collecting and hauling driftwood to the fires would get their blood pumping. He also sent out scouts to keep watch for any dangers that might threaten them from overland. Then he allowed the crews to dry themselves and their gear by the fires, giving everyone a cup of ale for the mourning of Hossig Sohossig. Niers Sodjernen put on his robes of Hondrig and led them through the *Cleaving Rite*, twice, for Kindron only allowed the crews their cups and prayer in shifts, with some men guarding the boats while others replaced the scouts looking over the plain from atop the cliffs. The men accepted their orders with a seriousness that - more than anything else - told the newest Sea Wolves that they were in Fjordland no longer.

While the mood had changed, some elements of their new routine remained the same: mourning or not, Kindron sent the four young Arctic Wolves to the boat with Yens for their usual session learning Straelish words. The longboats were rafting, lashed together and anchored by *Thunderer*. The prows of three longboats cast a shadow on the calm water in the light of a waxing moon; three shadowy beasts leaping towards the shore.

When Yens finally left them, they savoured the peacefulness of the place, looking out to sea or up to the cove's cliffs. Finally Lars looked across at Cairn and asked, "How in Hondrig's Sacred Name did you stay in the boat when that wave hit us?"

Cairn laughed, replying, "Ask 'in Rulla's Name,' not Hondrig's. She dealt my fate."

"Did She deal you that length of rope as well?" asked Thay with a grin. Lora and Lars looked at Thay with furrowed brows, their confusion evident. "Ach, sure he tied himself to his rowing bench. He wouldn't have been tossed out of *Rignil* had Hondrig Himself thrown her to Horoth."

Lars and Lora turned their gaze to Cairn and stared at him. They burst out laughing at the precise moment that Cairn turned and punched Thay in the arm, swearing, "*Skeetze!*"

"*Foxt!*" Thay replied instantly, without thought.

"Hondrig's Balls, Thay! That bit of rope saved your worthless life today!"

Thay squawked in pain and flopped over out of reach of a follow-up attack, but he laughed as he did so. Lora leaned forward giggling, her auburn hair falling in front of her face, and said, "But Cairn! Kindron would have had you gutting and scaling fish for the rest of the voyage if he knew you couldn't jump to one of his orders instantly. What were you thinking?"

"I was thinking it's been a long time since Kindron ordered me to do anything but pull on that Rulla-cursed oar!" Cairn replied. "What's more, I knew that something was going to happen to us. I could feel it in my bones."

"So could I," said Lora, and suddenly no one was laughing. She stared into the Godspace and, at length, added, "He knew it too. Hossig knew! That's the worst of it. He didn't know when it would happen, but he knew it would happen." The others had long-since learnt not to question Lora's uncanny knowledge on such matters. "What drives a man to carry on even when he knows what he's doing will claim him in the end?"

"Sure, we all know we're going to Hondrig one day," Lars replied, slinging his braid of white-blonde hair over his left ear even as Thay and Cairn cast their eyes out to sea. "It was surely a measure of Hossig's bravery that he carried on. It is the Fjordlander way; it always has been."

"So is that why we're carrying on with this voyage?" asked Lora. "Because our people always have done so?"

Cairn shifted his gaze from the dark sea, looking into Lora's eyes, and asked, "What's going to happen Lora? Something bad?"

Lora took her turn staring out to sea, but then she finally nodded. "Aye. Something's going to happen, but I don't know what."

"What about that impression of Asgear you told us about?" asked Lars, his blue eyes gleaming. "You know, the one about sensing something 'long, enduring and close'. That's bound to be a good omen, no?"

She shook her head. "I don't know, Lars, honestly I don't. That impression's still there, but it's still all twisted." She looked back from the sea, her eyes lighting upon Thay.

Lars declared, "You see true, Lora. I know you do! It's just like the stories of old Helgya, who foresaw a king among us. That's a fine future, no? I say it's not bad for us."

Lora nodded. "Thank you, Lars. You're right. It might not be bad for all of us."

Later, after being relieved, they went to the fires and lifted a mug in Hossig's memory.

Chapter Four

The fleet struck due east the following morning, and slowly they drew away from the mainland as the shoreline curved northwards. The winds blew strongly from the west, filling their sails, so they made good headway and did not need to row except to help in changing heading. With the Teeth shrinking from view behind them, the young Sea Wolves grew curious about the lands past which they sailed. They pressed Krüllig for answers and even Lora left Kindron's side to learn from their seasoned colleague.

"Yon lands are no-man's lands," he said, pointing to the receding shoreline. "Wild lands. They be dangerous, 'tis said. Who knows what beasts or devil-creatures like the *tosk-hyr* inhabit such places? The Boldring Mountains aren't a single wall, though I dare say Cairn knows as much, having spent his summers living on their shoulders. There's three broad chains what run south to the sea, though Hondrig be praised only one of 'em juts into the sea itself. I've heard tell of wild men what live in between 'em, though I don't imagine the tales are true.

"Further on there's a folk what call themselves the Veneg, but we call 'em the Fleelings, for they do naught but flee into the woods when they see us coming. And they don't got much, neither. Truth be told, they got so little we'd likely just ask for a dry roof over our heads if they didn't run off all the time. Worst of it is they usually burn their huts first. They be strange folk."

"Sounds like they know how to deal with us," Thay observed.

Krüllig chuckled and replied, "Perhaps they do, at that. After the Veneg the land gets gentler. Easier to raise cattle, grow grain and what not. So the people there have towns worth sacking. There's the Driga, the Straelings, and the Moortok, all one after the other along the coast. There's also the Polgati and the Catagenians to the north of 'em, just before the Drover lands."

"The Drovers, they're the nomad horse-herders Kyre would sing about?" asked Lars.

"Aye, that's them, though they herd reindeer too. I only sailed up there once - up the big river they call the Peregrinswater - and they were at its banks at one of their fairs. They had their painted wagons, and their fine dancing horses, their reindeer and their beautiful dark-skinned women, but they also had their long, curved swords, so there was no pillaging to be done. Besides, there was ten of 'em to each of us. Would'a loved one of 'em fine horses, though."

"Sure, what would you have done with a horse?" asked Lora, laughing.

"Paid me *lifgyld* ten years sooner's what!" Krüllig laughed. "No Sea Wolf captain, nor any other clan chief I know, could not covet such a beast. I'd be a made man."

"What about the other places?" asked Cairn. "What's worth pillaging there? And what of the women? Are they worth carrying off?" Lora slapped him across the back of the head, but he laughed and declared, "Whether you approve of it or not, Lora, I'm going to build myself a herd of women!"

"A harem," Krüllig said. "Erig sings about such things in some land far to the south. He says they be called harems."

"A harem, then," Cairn said. "I like the sound of that. Tell me about the women, Krüllig."

"Don't know much about women, lad, least of all foreign ones. All I know's they complicate things." This time it was Krüllig's turn to receive one of Lora's slaps across the back of the head. He hunched his shoulders against any potential follow-up attack and gave Lora a sheepish grin. When he was satisfied as to his safety, he continued, "As for the pillage, well, those lands are proper kingdoms and whatever we take will be hard-won, I don't doubt. But don't get your head full of notions about pillage just yet. We'll start by raiding the coast, I reckon, to make sure they have no boats of their own what can come after us. Pillage'll come after."

§

Norrgi sent them good winds for the next three days and they sped over the seas beyond sight of the shore. Every now and then Kindron would give command of *Rignil* to his burly blonde first officer, Asgear, leaving Lora to do the drumming whenever the wind died down and the crew broke out the oars. The Sea Wolf chieftain would go across either to *Thunderer* or *Northern Fire* and confer with their commanders, Toftig and Albig. "What do you suppose they're talking about?" asked Lora of Asgear once when all three captains were on *Thunderer*. "Where to strike first?" They were making headway under just their sail again, giving the rowers a rest and Lora a reprieve from the drum.

Asgear arched an eyebrow at her and shook his head, his shoulder-length blonde hair swirling back and forth. "Wonderin' about the concerns of the captains will get you a different sort of special treatment than the type you've been enjoyin' since you came on board." He pulled at the rudder, shifting their heading to see if he could catch the wind better. Once he satisfied himself with their headway, he added, more gently, "But you're likely right enough."

Indeed, once Kindron had jumped aboard again, the captains started issuing orders and the fleet separated, with *Thunderer* heading north by northeast, *Rignil* heading northeast, and *Northern Fire* bearing further towards the east again. Kindron left Asgear at the rudder and Lora noticed that he studied each man of his crew.

The following morning, Kindron beckoned Lars and Krül-lig to the stern and, to her astonishment, sent Lora and Asgear to replace them on the oars. As she settled into her new task, she heard Cairn snickering in front of her. "And just what do you find so amusing, Cairn Soleigh?" she snapped.

"You, girl," Cairn replied, laughing now. "It's about time you grew some callouses on those delicate hands of yours."

"Delicate hands? I'll have you know I've pulled more oars than you, sheep-herder!"

"Sure, you've spent too much time with our beloved captain, Lora," Thay chimed in. "You're starting to sound like him. Allow poor Cairn his mirth, this is the first morning he's rowed without griping about it!" Cairn didn't bother replying, instead he simply gave Thay a backhanded wallop to the head.

"What do you suppose they're discussing?" Lora asked, preempting any further fighting. Asgear broke the silence that followed, "He's giving them orders for the boardin'."

"The boarding?"

"Aye, the boardin'. If we're scoutin' out harbours to see what fightin' boats might have been built over the last year, then we're not likely to catch anyone by surprise by sailing *Rignil* into their waters, now, are we? No, we'll take the first small fishing boat we spy and those two will sail it closer to land."

"Why those two?" Thay asked.

"They're oar mates already, so they know how to get along together. Lars seems to know how to handle a boat and Krüllig certainly does. And when it comes to a fight or to razing a vessel, Krüllig knows what he's about. It also gives the captain a chance to take the measure of a new crewman."

When Lora and Asgear returned to their places a little while later, Lora could not help but feel envy at Lars' wide grin and the gleam in his eye.

§

Rignil found its prey just before nightfall. It was a small, single-sailed skiff manned by three fisherman struggling to untangle a net before dark set in. When one of them looked up into the gloom of the dusk and saw the rearing form of the wolf at the longboat's prow, he unleashed a desperate cry. The fishers cut loose the net and brought their vessel about. By the time they had run up their sail and were making headway, *Rignil* was already within bowshot. They closed the distance to the fishing vessel quickly and the four Sea Wolves closest to the prow stowed their oars and grabbed their axes. The small boat attempted a few last-ditch manoeuvres to elude the Fjordlanders, but if they thought their craft was nimbler than *Rignil*, they were mistaken. Kindron ordered some precise rowing and heaved on the rudder a couple of times, and the longboat came alongside the skiff. Grappling hooks ended the flight. Four Sea Wolves leapt into the fishing vessel. Bjarni took one swing of his axe at the man at the rudder, hitting him squarely in the temple and throwing him overboard. The other two fishermen threw themselves at their attackers' feet and begged for their lives in a language that Lars found strange. Lars wondered at the methodical boarding; the Sea Wolves didn't cheer or roar, they just went about their business.

As the men were hauled before Kindron, Krüllig tapped Lars on the arm and they clambered into the skiff. Krüllig collected the lines for the sail while Lars shipped the oars and pushed off from *Rignil*. "Here," Asgear said, tossing Krüllig a skin. "Whale oil." Krüllig nodded and took up the rudder. They set off due north just as the last light of dusk faded from the sky.

Lars said nothing to his oar mate as they ploughed through the waves. He knew that noise carried across water and he did not want to betray any nervousness to his seasoned colleague. But a hundred questions seized his mind: What language did those men speak? Did Krüllig understand it?

Why didn't Kindron kill them? Where were they from? Had Krüllig ever been there before? How big was their settlement? Was it well-defended? How did Krüllig know to sail due north from where *Rignil* intercepted the boat? He shook his head and crawled to the prow to look for torch light or for the black shapes of other ships against the night sky.

Not long afterwards, the waning moon rose above the eastern horizon, throwing a ghost-light pillar of reflection across the sea and illuminating the shoreline to the north of them. And as they neared the land, Lars did indeed see the light of a dozen lanterns sitting on people's window sills. He gestured north by northeast with his arm and then felt Krüllig steer the boat accordingly. Once the course was set, Lars took down the small sail to avoid its being seen in the moonlight. Then he set the oars, muffling them with strips of fur they had brought from *Rignil* and he established a steady rhythm to cross the remaining water between them and the harbour.

As they crept near the sheltered cove, Lars stowed the oars and allowed their little skiff to glide closer. He saw a breakwater emerge from the dark, obscuring murk of the cliffs behind. Holding onto the gunnel, Lars slid overboard into the water and fought to find his footing on the slippery boulders. He clambered up the breakwater and secured a rope to one of the upper stones.

Krüllig came up beside him and passed him *Harbinger* before climbing up to the summit of the breakwater. Lars crept up beside his oar mate and peeked into the sheltered harbour. There, bobbing quietly in the calm water behind the rocky wall, were a half-dozen fishing boats like the one they had sailed to shore. A long crescent shaped pebble beach gave way to an orderly collection of stucco and beam houses, each one as big as Toftig's Tower and featuring three rows of narrow windows, each one above the other. Krüllig grunted softly and pointed to the other end of the strand, where Lars saw the shape of a large vessel sitting perched in a dry dock.

"So, it's true," Krüllig stated. Lars could but guess what his oar mate meant and how Krüllig had become party to the news.

Krüllig gestured with his head and they crept back down to the boat. "Are we not going to destroy it?" Lars asked.

As Krüllig clambered over to the rudder, he replied, "Aye, but we can hardly stroll along yon strand there, build ourselves a cozy bonfire, and then stroll back now, can we? No, we'll put in up the coast and come overland. Cast off."

Lars rowed them straight out to sea until they were out of sight of the shore, whereupon he ran up the sail. Krüllig steered them east for a while, then northeast. They quickly found the cliffs again and followed the shoreline until they came to a small cove with a shallow stony beach. As Lars tied up the boat, Krüllig found them a path that wound its way up the cliff face.

They set out west at a jog over the gently rolling hills, keeping to the open areas between the copses of trees. The first sign that they neared the village was an empty shepherd's hut at the end of a wooded defile that dropped down to the beach, cutting a gap into the cliffs from which a narrow stream ran to the sea. They followed the stream down to the strand, keeping to the edge of the trees and watching for movement. When they got to the bottom of the defile, they crouched down behind a fallen tree and scanned the strand.

Again, they caught sight of the ship's frame, and then they noticed two huddled shapes sitting in the lee of a large stack of lumber. Krüllig nudged Lars - and Lars caught the meaning right away because he was already thinking about how two raiders walking along the strand or rowing into the harbour would have been spotted easily in the moonlight. Krüllig unhooked his axe, pulled his round shield off his back, and freed up his waterskin. Lars unsheathed *Harbinger* and adjusted his own shield, but before he could ask about the waterskin, Krüllig did something that Lars could never have foreseen. The bushy-bearded Sea Wolf stood, clambered over the fallen tree, and strode forward singing a Fjordlander song.

Lars followed, cursing Krüllig silently and wondering why they had thrown away any surprise they might have had. The men by the dry dock heard the song, stood, and called out something that was obviously a challenge. From his short time learning words from Yens, the Straeling captive back on *Rignil*, Lars thought the words were Straelish but he couldn't be sure, never having spent much time with Aganas back in Krannogberg and his time spent with Yens after the nightly sparring sessions helping less than he would have hoped.

Krüllig kept singing until the men repeated their challenge, whereupon he called back. This time Lars recognized the Straelish words "lost" and "help." The challenge was repeated a third time. The men had lifted swords, but the Sea Wolves had kept walking and had reached the beach. The clatter of their feet on the stone beach answered Lars' question about surprise and he kept his eyes fastened on a large bell hung from the girders of the dry dock, wondering when the men would reach over and sound the alarm.

Krüllig said something in reply to the challenge - Lars thought it might have included "Calm, friends," - and then he chuckled. The men seemed to relax, though Lars noted they did not set down their swords. As they neared, Krüllig tossed a waterskin to the man furthest from him, but nearest the bell, and gestured over his shoulder with his hand, saying, "My son." Each step brought them closer and Lars kept his eyes fixed on the man fumbling with the waterskin. The man unstopped the skin and held it to his nose. That was when Krüllig sprang at them, lunging at the man closest to him.

Lars hurtled at the man with the waterskin. The Straeling dropped the skin and returned his sword to his right hand, but the young Sea Wolf thrust *Harbinger*, catching the man in the shoulder. Lars heaved on his blade, spun through his first swing in one fluid movement, and sliced the man's neck on the second pass, cutting off the Straeling's cry of agony. He glanced at Krüllig in time to see his oar mate knock a sword from the other man's grasp and embed his axe deep into his opponent's back as the man turned to flee.

Krüllig spun to Lars and snapped, "Don't gawk, lad. Get a fire going before someone comes to find out what the shouting was all about!" Lars did just that, setting *Harbinger* aside and scrambling around the dry dock for kindling. He quickly built a conical stack right beneath the freshly tarred planks of the ship's hull. Krüllig emptied his skinful of whale oil on the wood. "Get it going, lad," Krüllig urged, "Someone's coming."

Lars pulled out his flint and steel, and struck one against the other, throwing sparks at his pile, but it did not catch. He heard shouting from down the strand and was aware of Krüllig waving. Suddenly the oil caught the spark and flames sprang to life. The shouting from the strand exploded in intensity. Krüllig tossed a couple of burning brands inside the ship and said, "Good lad. Now it's time to go!" Lars gathered up *Harbinger* and his shield and off they ran, darting across the beach and up the path beside the stream. At the top of the defile, Lars looked over his shoulder and saw a raging bonfire around the prow of the ship and silhouetted figures flitting about it like moths around a tallow on midsummer's night.

They ran like devils overland to the cove. Gasping for breath, Lars untied their mooring line, pushed them off, and flopped into the skiff. "Catch your breath after ..." Krüllig panted, "... after you've got the sail fixed." Lars nodded and trimmed the sail as Krüllig turned them about. Later, they saw the light of a fire in the north as they sailed away from land to their rendezvous with *Rignil*, and then they spotted other beacon fires spring up and down the coastline. "Well," said Krüllig with a grin, "we'll likely have to sail for leagues on end before we catch anyone else by surprise with our wee summer raid. Least we taught them a lesson about protecting their boats. You did well, lad."

Lars grinned in the light of the moon. His first raid was a success.

§

Early the next evening, *Rignil* joined *Thunderer* again and they sailed east through the night. Word came to them from Toftig's crew of an uneventful sailing. The port town that they had investigated had nothing more than a few fishing boats and one small trading vessel sitting too high in the water to have much interesting cargo in its hold.

By noon the next day, they met Albig's *Northern Fire* and the three vessels rafted while their captains and first officers conferred. To Lora's surprise, no one told her to make herself scarce as they gathered around Kindron.

Albig reported that the two settlements his Sea Wolves had scouted only had fishing vessels and little enough wealth from the looks of them. Both sets of scouts had returned without engaging anyone and, hopefully, without being seen. They had kept out of sight of land and had avoided any contact with vessels as they waited for the other ships to rendezvous.

Kindron beckoned for Krüllig to come forward then and give a first-hand account of his and Lars' attack. When Krüllig had finished his tale, Albig said, "We saw the beacon fires lit from the west and carrying on east. That's as sure a sign as any that these lands aren't at war with each other this year. Still, we fired the only threat to us hereabouts."

Kindron nodded and added, "Mind, I reckon these parts won't be surprised by a summer sailing again. They'll learn to keep their eyes open, their weapons at hand and their ships better protected. With the beacons lit, we'll have to sail further east yet."

Jurgen, *Northern Fire's* first officer ended a short silence by asking, "The Empire?"

Albig, Jurgen's skipper, shook his head, "We'd need to know a lot more about the lay of the land to bother them."

"What about sailin' up the Peregrinswater?" offered Asgear.

Toftig, *Thunderer's* skipper, nodded and said, "We haven't paid our respects to the Catagenians or the Polgati for a few years. It would be far from the coast so there wouldn't be a worry about them receiving news of us from the beacons."

Albig shook his head again and said, "We're off the Straelish coast. We should put some people ashore first to learn the flow and the eddies of the north kingdoms. If the Catagenians have been warring with the Moortok or the Straelings, or amongst themselves, then we'd be sailing into a right fucking mess."

"We put people ashore and the game's up," declared Kurg, *Thunderer's* first officer. "It's not like we're good at blending in. Who of us speaks Straelish well enough to pass as a native? One of us; Yens. He still doesn't love us yet and we've only had him in shackles for three years."

"Whoever we put ashore don't have to recite a saga," snapped Albig. "Most Driga speak a form of Straelish and you've got two Driga prisoners, Kindron, from that boat. Why not offer the pair of them their freedom if one goes ashore for us? You could hold the other for assurance."

"He could spew out whatever lies he wanted and we'd not know better," said Toftig.

"We could put someone ashore with him," Albig replied.

"Still have the problem about being identified," said Toftig. "Who could we put ashore who wouldn't be a giveaway?"

"Me!" interjected Lora. Silence followed as seven seasoned Sea Wolves turned steely eyes to her. But Lora did not wilt. "Sure, what have you brought me along for if not to put me to good use? I can pose as his daughter. If he crosses us ..." She pulled out her seax: "Meet *Iss*, here. If he plays us false, he'll meet it too." It was a fine weapon and it duly impressed the Sea Wolves with its sweeping curves and icicle-like runic markings along the top.

"Do you really speak Straelish, lass?" asked Jurgen. "Learning a few begrudged words every day from Yens doesn't mean you can speak a tongue. Like as not he's been lying to you, teaching you Hondrig only knows what. He has no love for us. We put you in with one of those prisoners and sure you'd never know what the man said."

"I learnt my first Straelish words when I was young, back home," she retorted. Then she looked Kindron in the eye and said, "You must remember Gunder Sohargar. He mustered out of the Arctic Wolves with our chieftain, Knab."

"Your former chieftain," Kindron corrected her. "You're an Arctic Wolf now. And yes, I do mind old Gunder. What of him?"

"Don't you remember his wife, Aganas? She's a Straeling: long, curly dark hair flowing all about her face."

"Ah yes, now I mind her. Handsome woman."

"Well, she used to teach me and Thay. Both of us are far ahead of Cairn and Lars. Ask Yens. Better yet, ask Krüllig." Krüllig nodded to that.

Albig arched an eyebrow at Krüllig, "You know Straelish?"

"A little bit," the bushy-bearded Sea Wolf replied. "A very little bit. But before you get thinking about putting me ashore, take a good look at me. How much do I look like a Straeling?"

Kindron laughed and slapped his crewman on the back, "Right enough. We shave that there beard of yours and you'd still look half bear. No, a Straeling, you're not."

"I'll do double lessons with Yens," Lora declared. "How long will it take us to sail to this Peregrinswater? I'll certainly know enough by then to get by." Then, turning to Kindron, she added, "And then you'd not have to rely on prisoners or half-bears to go ashore in the future."

Kindron laughed even harder. "Right enough, lass. I wouldn't. It's decided. We put you ashore at the Peregrinsmouth! I'm tempted to put one of your chums ashore with you, though, to make sure you can sleep without being stuck, yourself, by our guest's dagger."

§

Kindron had the Sea Wolf Priest of Hondrig, Niers Sodjernen, bear witness to a pact he struck with the two new Driga prisoners with Yens' help translating; he would give them their freedom if they served well in one short task. The men readily agreed when they heard what it was their captors wished of them; guiding Lora into a Straelish village.

Therefore, as the ships sailed further and further east, Lora and Thay spent much of the next three days with Yens at the prow of the ship. Without Cairn and Lars holding them back in their lessons, they made good progress in how to hold a conversation in Straelish. Yens seemed less hostile, being free of the rowing, and was a less truculent teacher as a result. When Thay was sent to an infrequent shift on the oars, he was surprised to find that Cairn and Lars, too, were learning more Straelish, though not as quickly. Jealous of Lora and Thay, they had pressed Krüllig for instruction after learning he had picked up pidgin Straelish during a year as a captured slave with the Driga.

By the fourth day, Lora and Thay could hear the impact of those days in their childhood with Aganas, as well as both their time with Yens and now with the new prisoners. They could hold their own in a conversation as long as it avoided hypothetical situations, and their accent was more than passable, especially if they were to be taken for Driga. The fleet changed bearing from due east to north by northeast. Their luck held and they did not see any other vessels - vessels that could fly before them and raise an alarm. *Rignil* left the other two boats behind and sped north under both sail and oar while Kindron readied the expedition with gear and final instructions. Before nightfall they came to the Peregrinsmouth, a wide marshy estuary teeming with bird life and all the cacophony that comes with such a place. They climbed into the boat's dinghy with the fortunate prisoner, Jax Netman, and Kindron bade them good luck. *Rignil* did not linger to see them off, though. She came about, trimmed her sail and sped off south into the lingering dusk with a strain of Erig's strumming on the harp wafting back to them over the dark water. Lora recognized the tune, *"Fare Well Daughter."*

Thay rowed Lora and Jax ashore to the shrill cries of redwinged blackbirds and trumpeter swans. He found a bit of solid ground after rowing upstream through the deepening dusk and then covered the rowboat with reeds. Thay and Lora hoisted packs of their "father's" trade goods - all-weather skins from the north - and followed Jax as he picked a way through the marsh. It took until midnight before they emerged from the reeds and the watery channels to reach dry ground. Then Lora ordered a rest until dawn.

"Do we need to tie you up or will you keep to your word?" Lora asked Jax in Straelish, a language the man understood.

"I have promised your skipper and my kinsman's life depends on me keeping my faith."

Lora glanced at Thay. "Do we trust him?" she asked, keeping to Straelish, for they had decided to get into the habit of speaking it on the off chance that later they might get overheard. Jax's muttered something to himself in his Driga tongue in response to Lora's query.

"What'd you say?" Thay asked, his tone firm but not unkind.

Jax nigh on snarled his reply, "I said 'barbarous thorn people,' for that's what you are!"

"Thorn people?" Thay repeated.

"It's what people hereabouts name you ... for you're all like thorns, pricking us, drawing blood, spreading pain."

Thay glanced at Lora. "He's tired and he's frightened, but he knows he's one day of loyal service from freedom. He'll keep his word." Jax huffed and stretched himself out to sleep. Lora and Thay took turns keeping watch.

They carried on again at first light, finding the main channel of the Peregrinswater and then following its west bank north. They passed a smattering of isolated farmsteads before arriving at the town, that Jax called Marshton Vale, at midday. During the march, Lora and Thay marvelled at the size of the fields, huge swaths of wheat glowing amber in the sun and swaying in the light breeze. "I've not seen its like," Thay whispered to Lora in his Straelish.

Indeed, Jax did overhear and asked, "Not seen what? Fields? Do you folk do naught but visit misery on others? Do you feed your sheep stolen coin?"

"Keep a civil tongue in your head!" Lora snapped. After that they proceeded in silence, but Thay could not shake Jax's remarks from his head until they came to Marshton Vale.

When they entered the town, the two Fjordlanders saw the two and three story houses that Lars had described from his raid. The houses most often had white painted stucco walls cross-hatched by dark wooden beams with shuttered windows and steep-sloped roofs of clay tiles. There were more people than Thay or Lora had ever seen in one place, and there were a great many beasts of burden. Thay wondered if the horses he saw were the fabled Drover horses of which Krüllig spoke so highly.

"We should go to the town square, if there is one, and see if anyone wants these skins," Jax suggested. "If there's gossip about, we should be able to get it out of those we deal with."

Lora nodded and they followed the flow of people into the heart of town. She noticed that the townsfolk watched them with interest, but with no apparent alarm. A beardless lad and a russet-haired maiden travelling with an older man who clearly did not look like a warrior raised no concern for these people. Jax wasted no time getting on with his mission, taking them across a small common space where women sold fruits and vegetables spread out on blankets on the ground. Thay noticed a couple of buildings around the common that were as broad as the roundhouse in Krannogberg, but that reached up two or three stories. Jax took them to one of these, into a place that seemed to do nothing but trade in hard goods. Thay looked around the shop, wide eyed, thinking it was like a Summer Festival day in Narhaven. By the time he had walked around and looked at everything that was on sale, Jax had already sold the skins, the quality of which seemed to impress the shopkeeper. "Daughter," Jax said, beckoning Lora over to him, "These are for our purse," and he passed a handful of coin to her, which she took time to study, having seen few examples of such minted wealth before.

They made a great show of lunching in the common beside some of the women selling lettuce, carrots and turnips. Jax ended up in a lively chat with two of the women. They talked about the summer weather, traffic on the Peregrinswater, and finally, the resolve of the people in this part of the world to be ready for the winter raiders if they dared come. "They're interested in naught but destruction," declared one of the women. "They never come for commerce or any such useful purpose. They only trade in death and fire. They'll amount to naught in the end."

"Aye, right enough" Jax agreed, casting a sidelong look at Thay. "I doubt they build much in their lands."

Talk then passed on to other subjects. The Queen of the Straelings, it seemed, had raised taxes and duties in order to strengthen the country's defences and to build a new basilica in her mother's birthplace, a town called Shipton. Jax asked about the defences while Thay pondered what "basilica" meant, finally coming to the conclusion it must be a grand place for thrashing wheat. Jax seemed to ask the minimum questions needed to fulfill the mission, but Lora probed further and no one seemed to think her anything but the young Driga woman she pretended to be. She discovered that Straeland had struck a peace treaty with Moortovia across the river and with Drigaland to the west.

They discovered little else of any evident use and took their leave of Marshton Vale by mid-afternoon. Lightened of their load of skins, they made better time and found their row boat well before dusk. Thay had rowed them out of the marsh by nightfall. Lora lit their shuttered lantern and stayed at the prow, directing its light out to sea while Thay and Jax each took an oar.

Rignil retrieved them before midnight. Once on board, Kindron bid them get some rest before morning and he ordered his ship south to meet up with *Thunderer* and *Northern Fire*.

§

Lora awoke just before dawn as the three ships of the Fjordlander fleet were manoeuvring into rafting order. Once the three vessels were lashed together, the captains and first officers asked her for a full report. She told them what she had heard and finished by giving them her opinion, ignoring the fact the no one had asked her for it. "They've struck a peace and have the money now to consider an enemy they obviously hate. If we sail up that river, we can't hide like we can here on the high seas. My guess is that you'll find eyes watching our progress and a welcoming party wherever we put ashore."

As before, Kindron remained quiet and let his officers wage the debate. Asgear and Jurgen suggested that peace among the kingdoms bode well for an attack up the Peregrinswater because Straeland and Moortovia would be less watchful of the great river that formed the border between the two kingdoms. Albig remained suspicious of such a sailing and pushed for a coastal raid on the Moortok. Albig liked the idea of attacking the Polgati and the Catagenians and thought that the risks of taking the great river might be avoided by portaging over the Straeng Headlands and by travelling by night. Kurg advocated raiding along the coast until other Sea Wolf clans could join them in the autumn. Then, he said, they would have the strength to move up the river.

Kindron sent them back to their boats without betraying his thoughts. He ordered the fleet north and brought them to an isolated cape west of the Peregrinsmouth. There he ordered the prisoners' fishing boat be beached and three holes be drilled into its hull. Then he left them materials to make repairs and said to them, with Yens translating, "You've served us well and we honour our pledge to you. You are free now, but you'll find a wee problem if your intent is to raise these lands against us. That should allow us time to get well ahead of you before you can make much mischief. Take my advice. Go straight home."

Kindron had the fleet sail further west again before turning south and out of sight of shore. He had the fleet raft once more and he spoke to the Sea Wolves of his plan.

"I'd like to see this 'basilica' being built in Shipton. Krüllig tells me it's a holy place. Well, I've never seen any holy place that was short on treasure.

"It's also been a while since I paid Shipton a visit. It sits on the first large tributary of the Peregrinswater and has much of the Straelish trade with the outside world. It'll be a rich prize.

"But I think our dear Lora has the right of it - I don't think we can just sail up the Peregrinsmouth and hope no one sees us. We'll take Albig's advice. We'll sail up the Straeng, hump over its eastern headlands, and come down on Shipton from up river. They'll not think to look for us coming down out of the hills and I'm sure Niers will agree that our daring will entertain the Gods! ... certainly Tanat the Rogue! Now," Kindron commanded, "get your sails trimmed. We're sailing west. With Tanat's help, we'll soon be as rich as Florri Himself!"

Chapter Five

Rather than venture up the Straeng in daylight, Kindron took them to an isolated cove nearby to rest. At dusk, they loaded up the longboats and cast off, finding the mouth of the river well before midnight. Even though Florri favoured them with a southerly wind that allowed them to make headway under sail, they rowed as well, and quickly, great arms straining at the stout oars and thrusting the ships forward. They fell into a furious rhythm and, as though under a trance, maintained it even as Asgear stopped drumming. They rotated on the oars so as not to exhaust the crews, but they did not relent. They passed a hamlet on the east bank, dark and sleeping deeply, without anyone taking any notice of them. No dogs barked, no night watchmen lit beacons or sounded horns, and no fishermen banged oars off gunnels. Despite the urgency of the rowing, Thay did look up briefly and noticed one building standing larger among the others, with a tall, narrow tower, and he wondered what it was. Even after they rounded a bend in the river, the tower lurked over the tops of trees before receding slowly into the night.

By dawn they had come a goodly ways, only passing a few quiet, isolated farmsteads, and they hid themselves in a broad marsh they discovered under the moonlight. They took down their masts and posted guards in some trees on the riverbank to warn them of river traffic or snooping travellers. Kindron cursed them, told them they would have to row twice as hard the next night and threatened them all that he would have anyone who did not fall asleep instantly whipped, but he seemed well pleased with the progress they had made. The youngsters had no need of threats to force them to sleep. Even Lars and Thay, long used to rowing and hauling on fishing lines, were exhausted. Before falling into a deep slumber, Cairn muttered that his arms were made of stone and that he would have to get Krüllig to pick his nose for him. Krüllig, of course, ever there to defend and protect his shipmate, offered up one single finger.

Some while later, Thay awoke from sleep troubled by heat and glaring, late summer light. He looked about him and saw that the sun had climbed above the trees and was blazing down on him. All around, the others slept on, oblivious to the summer heat. He had the same feeling as he had when awaking from one of his crimson dreams, when the dragon showed herself to him. But he had no recollection of any image or words from his sleep. He got up, crept across to the boat's prow so not as to disturb anyone, and leapt to the dry shore. He waved to the trees where he saw the scouts watching him as he clambered up the riverbank. He sat there, gazing at the rich land around him and gave himself over to his daydreaming.

Although he had only seen the Demon's Teeth and now this land of the Straelings, he understood immediately the allure of raiding that ran in Fjordlander blood. These were fertile lands, their bounty vast in comparison with that offered by the high pastures or the stark fjords of his home. Tall trees, taller even than those in the Harrowood, lined the riverbank and were scattered over the flood plain. He also recognized apple trees, just like the one in the sheltered courtyard of Narhaven only much bigger, in the hedge rows that separated the tilled fields of this country. The fields themselves were bursting with golden wheat. One field was teeming with more cattle than he had ever seen in one place before. He lost himself in imaging having a household in such a place, a mighty thane presiding over a wealthy estate with a beautiful woman at his side. Something in his mind - something related to his earlier dream - told him: you will be able to choose such a life. Something else told him Hondrig, the Judge - would render the Last Judgement on him, for good or ill, based on his choice.

Suddenly a hand clamped onto his shoulder and Thay gave a jump. Behind him, Borath, one of the scouts, laughed at his reaction. "Settle down lad! I'm done my watch and there's no point in waking another man to relieve me if you're so intent on lollygagging during your sleep time. I'm not so sure I should send you up yon tree, though, if you didn't notice me coming up to you. Watch is for watching, not drooling on your shirt!"

Thay took a breath and then said, "Take your rest, Borath. I'll go on up and keep my wits about me." He took care not to lose himself in thought again that morning.

§

Kindron had little need to rouse the Sea Wolves at the end of the afternoon, most were already up and about after having slept well during the day. Some woke with sunburns on their necks and arms, and Cairn voiced another complaint to Lars, "Now I've got baked stone for arms!"

Kindron had already dispatched runners to range ahead on both banks to ensure that no one would spy the fleet's passing and Lora was one of these, for she could run quickly over long distances. Also, if the worst came to pass and she were taken prisoner, she knew the language enough that she felt confident she could convince anyone that she was an errant Driga daughter fleeing an abusive stepfather. So off she ran along the east bank, cutting over the narrow shoulders of land that forced the Straeng to meander in lazy loops as it flowed to the sea.

Although she saw crops ripening in narrow fields, and sheep and cattle grazing on bright green grass, she saw neither any settlement nor any person near the river. She wondered whether people came to the Straeng like her people did to the Tallog River back home, to harness its wealth only in certain seasons when the salmon passed or when the trout were fat. She tied her markers to suitable trees, long red ribbons looped to branches that arched over the water that the crews could spot easily from down river, and she continued on over the next hilly shoulder between river bends.

She attached four such ribbons before sitting down on a high hillock at twilight and waited for *Rignil* to catch up to her. The fleet appeared at dusk, picked her and two other runners up, and plied on up river under the cover of darkness, when the risk of anyone sighting them diminished. Just after midnight they came to a confluence where a narrow, swift tributary met the Straeng from the east. They took this river and fought against the current, aided by a brisk west wind that filled their sails and drove their prows forward. Beside them, the fens and marshes of the lower Straeng gave way to steep banks and broad sloping fields that rose to tall hills on either side of them. They immediately saw greater evidence of settlement: a derelict quay sticking into the river from the north bank, a dark village - deep in sleep - huddled on the south bank, and a broad wooden bridge that forced them to take down their masts to pass underneath its span.

By the time a grey light grew in the eastern sky, they had travelled nigh on seven leagues. Kindron guided them to a part of the river where the current drove through a narrows and swirled back against a low cliff where there was a deep basin. The fleet anchored there and set scouts on the banks as the sun came up. They spent another day at anchor, first sleeping, then tending to the chores that inevitably came with boats, mending ropes, bailing out bilge water, driving horsehair and tarred wool in between leaky planks, replacing an oar lock, and cleaning the wolf head figures as the prows of the ships. Kindron ordered them to set out again in the golden light of the early evening. As dusk descended, they came to a sparkling sheet of shallow rapids and the heavy work began.

The portage over the rapids went quickly, though the work demanded much of them. They hauled down the masts of the ships as two teams of men fixed ropes to the prow of the first ship, *Rignil*. Then those teams of men hauled on the ropes while the bulk of the three crews hoisted *Rignil* onto their shoulders and walked it to deeper water at the head of the rapids. The portage was not far, just over a hundred paces, but neither was the way easy and it was a great struggle to haul the boat up one shelf of rock in particular. By the time they got *Rignil* back in the water, deep dark had fallen, complicating the portage for the other two vessels. But the crews had figured out the job and *Thunderer* took less time to heave and lug across, and *Northern Fire* took less time again. They were soon under sail once more, and the crews gave thanks to Norrgi, the Master of the Winds, for the stiffening breeze from the west that allowed them to give their sore arms a rest and proceed under sails.

The respite only lasted until the sky turned golden grey in the northeast very early in the morning when they came to a wide shallows. They had already been navigating around shoals and islets for some time before the hull of *Rignil* scraped the sandy bottom. "This is where the real hard work begins, lads," called Kindron. "From here we make overland southeast across yon saddle of land. Don't worry though, the slope is gentle on this side of the hill, and then we'll walk our ladies down into the headwaters of the Tamas. From there, we'll make good time down river to this basilica thing. Right, get to work!"

Fjordlander longboats were light enough that the crews had no need to unload the boats completely. Again, once they had pulled down the masts, two crews hoisted *Rignil* onto their shoulders while the other readied *Thunderer* for her portage, while a few runners, Lora and Lars included, scouted. As Kindron had said, the slope was manageable and they made good time. Cairn and Thay joined the crews in lugging the boat on their shoulders, and though it was a long way to slog, they found themselves far down the other side of the saddle between the hills when the sun peeked over the eastern horizon. Kindron allowed a short break and their priest, Niers Sodjernen, led them in a prayer to welcome a new day. Once they had beseeched Hondrig for strength, Rulla for protection, and Florri for good fortune, their labour continued, though now the challenge was to ensure that they did not let gravity do their work for them: it would not do for them to go careening off and somehow let *Rignil* fall from their grasp. Progress downhill was much quicker and soon Lora came running out of the dawn and reported where boats could put in to a tributary of the Tamas up ahead. They veered south, rounded a copse-shrouded knoll and found a long narrow lake in the valley beneath them.

By the time they eased *Rignil* into the reeds at the head of the lake, Cairn thought his arms would burst or that his back would snap suddenly. Kindron dispatched the men on the return leg but he spared Cairn the run. He took the big lad aside as the others caught their breath and though his words were typical, his tone was not unkind, "We need some guards at this end now, and I doubt you'll survive the run, fat pig that you are and all. As much as your arms have thickened, and gotten much redder, I must declare - I doubt you can heft another boat overland and still pull oars at the end of the day. But I've heard it said you can swing that maul of yours, so now's your chance to do something useful. Stay here with Asgear, Lora, and Bjarni and guard my beauty."

Cairn both resented the unsaid criticism and welcomed the respite for his arms. The assignment was not a rest, however, as Asgear soon had them stand oars on end and push against the bank, thrusting *Rignil* out into the middle of the lake. There they dropped anchor, playing the rope out to a surprising depth. "Good," Asgear said when they were done, "now anyone'll have to swim to us if they think us a morsel worth pluckin.'" Then to keep them busy he had them work getting the rigging and the oar locks in good repair. As they worked, Cairn looked up over the land to the west and marvelled at it; it looked soft, with thick grass blanketing soft rolling hills and lush, full trees breaking a monotony of emerald with rich browns and blossoms of white. The lands had none of the starkness of his home, but he did not begrudge them their beauty. Rather, he drank it in knowing that it was a rare luxury for such as him. He did not know why, but something told him his fate would not let him enjoy the fruits of such a place. His was a darker, bloodier path.

Then he noticed movement.

Among the trees near the ridge that formed the northern boundary of the lake's water basin Cairn saw a flash of blue against the green landscape. "Asgear," he called out as quietly as he could while making sure the officer could hear him, "What do you make of yon stain of blue against the ridge line up there by those big trees?" He gestured with his chin, thrusting it towards the blue while keeping his hands working.

Asgear came over to him quickly, flailing his whip about as though to lash it across Cairn's broad back. "You lazy shit," he yelled, lashing the whip against the deck behind the youngster, though to someone watching from afar it may have seemed as though Cairn had been hit. Cairn flung back his head and yelled, colluding in the ruse. Then, he allowed his head to flop forward again. In a quiet voice Asgear asked, "Whaddya see?"

"Dunno," Cairn whispered, though he made it seem as though he panted in pain. "I thought I saw a flash of blue slip over the ridge and into those trees there." He pointed at Lora at the stern, but Asgear caught the real direction in Cairn's eyes.

"Get back to work you piece of dung!" Asgear yelled. Lora clambered across the deck to her friend to examine his supposed lash, but Asgear's hand dropped on her shoulder and threw her towards the prow. "Don't you go coddlin' our princeling here! He can manage. Mind your own work." Then he added in a whisper, "He's fine, I didn't touch him. Keep one of those fair eyes of yours lookin' for movement up on that ridge there, but don't let on you're doin' so."

She looked at him then and in her mind's eye she saw a ruined man with twisted hands instead of *Rignil's* strong first officer, and she saw her own hand entwined in one of those mangled hands. Disconcerted, she devoted herself to the tasks at hand. She stowed ropes, repaired locks, and fixed the yardarm, gazing all the while at Asgear. Kindron's first officer set himself to his own work, though he would shift his clear blue eyes up to the ridge line without moving his head. For the first time, she saw beyond the first officer's gruffness, took in his shoulder length, springy, blonde hair and the elegant way his long, braided moustaches hung onto his bushy beard.

Finally runners started arriving with the masts and those goods that had needed unloading from the vessels. They beached *Rignil* again and put Cairn to work loading and stowing goods as well as replacing deck boards. Cairn did note that Asgear sent three men creeping up to the woods. They returned not long afterwards, shaking their heads and shrugging. By noon, *Thunderer* and *Northern Fire* sat in the water and all the gear had been brought overland. Cairn did see Asgear speak to Kindron but whether the talk was of readiness or spies, the Sea Wolf chieftain simply nodded and ordered them to get under way.

§

Kindron ordered the crew to the oars and kept the sails furled. They drove down the river in single file, *Rignil* leading the way with Lora at the prow, pointing out shallows to Kindron at the rudder. They made good time - the river ran straight, swift and deep for many a league - and they only had to slow down to take soundings in the odd shallow channel. Cairn never had the time to speak his fears to his friends, but they made such good headway that he guessed Asgear had convinced Kindron to outrun any possible warning that locals might send. Indeed, Kindron drove his crews harder than he had since the Demon's Teeth. He didn't anchor anywhere, didn't send any runners off scouting and didn't allow any rests. When the wind did not blow from their backs, allowing them to make headway under sail, he made the crews row in alternate shifts, despite the fact that the current pushed them quickly eastwards. Through an entire night and day, Kindron did not allow any pause on shore or moment of idle drifting among the eddies, and they made quick progress, passing no noticeable villages or bridges or watchtowers. Cairn's unease eventually gave way to confidence as they swept past a solitary mill nestled on the right bank in the early morning of the second day from the lake without anyone spotting a sign of danger or anyone seeing any messenger's steed dart off overland.

They stopped for a rest at the end of that second day, sheltering in a cove on the north bank amongst tall reeds. The only mates on duty were the scouts positioned on the hills and in the largest trees near the fleet. Kindron had selected Thay to spend a watchful night looking after the vessels and the other three youngsters had a moment to talk before retiring for their rest. Cairn said, "We've made good time since we found this stream. Do you think anyone's the wiser?"

Lars chuckled and retorted, "Ach, never you worry! Sure you've got a grand notion of how Kindron works if you think he wants anyone to know who plucks their gold before he comes to pluck it! Of course not!"

Cairn nodded and replied, "Aye, right enough. He's not one for gettin' himself killed, I suppose." He noticed that Lora studied him and Lars as they talked.

"You just wait and see," Lars said. "This raid'll be the biggest thing that ever happened to us. Our names will be remembered because of it!"

"I hope you're wrong," Lora sighed before turning onto her bedroll and pretending to fall asleep.

§

Thay marvelled at the dawn colours as they crept over the horizon. He had always had a habit of letting his daydreams carry him away during the long hours on his father's boat, and as Kindron called the crews to the ships that morning, he remained enmeshed in a daydream of fleeting golden sparks - benevolent sprites, he told himself, who protected him - of crumbled gems, of lungs rejoicing from breathing fresh air, and of soaring dragons flying in a golden daybreak sky. Sitting up on the hillside above the cove, he had no idea that the fleet was already hauling anchor. One of his crimson dreams came, showing him a future of strife and war and anger and frustration. Yorsgall had to call to him to dislodge his reverie. Thay signalled to him, rose, and then walked haltingly to *Rignil*, rubbing feeling into his legs.

The fleet set sail shortly after Thay set foot again on *Rignil's* deck. As he took up his oar, Cairn grinned at him, "And what did the grand dreamer have to ponder this morning that he couldn't join us for a wee row down this charming river?"

Thay pulled on his oar, looked into Cairn's eyes and replied, "A troubled future, it seems." The reply surprised Cairn enough to shut him up until past midday, when they put in alongside a wooden bridge.

§

"No. You four stay," Kindron declared to Lars. He stood on shore with the crews of the three vessels around him. "I won't have my better hands looking after our boats. I can't spare them. You, however, I can spare. You're far from prime fighting age, but you can manage oars right enough. Stay here and guard the boats. Put them to flame if needs be, but don't, don't let them fall into the hands of our enemies. Don't fool yourself, guarding these boats is a great honour. They are everything to me."

"What about them," Lars prodded, pointing at the youths who had joined them from Sangspit. "Why do those damned Jarlags get to go?"

Kindron held a finger to Lars' forehead. "I warned you!" he hissed. "Those are Sea Wolves, just like you. They're your brothers." Then, for good measure, he used that finger to poke Lars in the chest.

Lars managed to pull himself erect again and muttered through clenched teeth a "But ..."

"No buts," Kindron said, with just the hint of a smile on his face. "Listen, I have decided. You had your chance to prove your worth and now I need to test their mettle. Follow your orders crewman! You will stay here and protect the boats. Keep them ready for sail, for we shall surely arrive with the wrath of these folk on our heels. I want you to safeguard our escape!"

Something seemed wrong, but yet also somehow right to Thay, and so he said nothing. In the end, they sat apart and watched their Priest of Hondrig, Niers, consecrate the mission. The holy man offered a prayer to Florri, the God of Good Fortune, and then one to Tanat the Rogue, in whose name they had planned the raid, all the while with Erig strumming soft strains on his harp. Niers offered a final blessing and the crews of the three ships strode off together leaving Lars, Lora, Thay, Cairn, and the chained crewman, Yens, to their fates.

After watching their oar mates cross over the ridge line above them, they sat for a while on *Rignil's* benches, close to Yens in case the Straeling tried to get up to some mischief in spite of the bonds that kept him chained to his bench. None said what was on their minds. That was when a dull rumble pricked Thay's ears and he glanced westwards, back up the river valley. He saw a renegade storm pushing an odd wall of cloud their way. Like thunderclouds, the wall of cloud crouched low on the land and towered high into the sky. Unlike thunder heads, the wall seemed boundless. Being on a river, there would be no sailing around this one; the fleet would have to shelter from it somewhere along the riverbank. Not only did the wall of cloud approach rapidly, it even appeared tinted with an eerie green hue. Thay had never seen such strange weather before, and he hoped he never would again.

For some reason, Thay wanted to light a fire. Given Kindron's order to them to light the boats if disaster should befall the raid, he figured his compulsion made good sense. He rose, hopped off the longboat and went to gather a bundle of kindling. He dropped it against *Rignil's* hull and gestured at the others to do the same. Cairn asked, "What about Yens?"

Thay shrugged and replied, "He's chained up and there's a good padlock holding fast the chains. What mischief can he really cause? Make sure there's nothing more dangerous than an oar lock near him and come on down. If he cries out or something, we can always climb back up and remind him to be good. Come on, let's get a small fire going just in case."

As Thay dropped his second bundle of wood on the growing pile, he noticed the eerie silence; no birdsong, no talking, just the odd rumble coming from the approaching storm. Thay glanced again to the west and he shook his head in wonder and alarm at the storm's progress. "Norrgi deliver us!" he whispered. The storm towered over the horizon, moving quicker than any weather he had ever seen. Waves of green sheet lightning rolled and slid underneath the dark, towering clouds that consumed the sky. The tall grass on the slopes around them bent with the rising wind.

He crossed to *Northern Fire* and suddenly the wind buffeted him with a vengeance. It swirled around and made them don their cloaks. By now the Godspace had turned ink black except for those eerie green rolling waves of light that seemed to grow from the middle of the cloud and then slowly crawl underneath the ominous canopy. With Cairn acting as a wind block - one of his natural talents - Thay got a blaze lit and held his hands to the flames for warmth. Cairn, too, knelt close to the fire and sighed, "Ah, that's better. You know, I didn't actually enjoy having frozen, baked stone arms."

Thay chuckled and shook his head. "*Skeetze*," he said.

"*Foxt*," Cairn instantly replied.

At that moment, they heard a cry and all turned their heads to see Krüllig running over the lip of the rise to the north. "Fire the boats!" he yelled as he hurtled over the hill and came pounding down towards them. "Fire the boats!"

Lora was the first to react. "Hondrig's Cock!" she cursed, She spun and faced the boys, yelling, "I'll take *Thunderer!*" She grabbed a brand from the fire and ran to the furthest longboat.

Cairn called out a question over the wind, "Can we not take a boat and flee?"

Lars, returning from collecting kindling, answered, "We've no crew!" He looked up to see his oar mate streaking down the hill and felt a chill creep up his spine; there were no other Sea Wolves following. Lars had come to know Krüllig; a man always ready to share his wisdom or humour. All he saw now in Krüllig's features was fear, but at that very moment, the older man's face changed. He slowed and looked at the youths doing their best to obey him, and then he turned around. "Where are the others?" Lars called out.

Then Lars saw thirty Straelings emerge over the lip of the hill, not forty paces behind. Krüllig drew his axe from his belt and charged back up the slope. Lars cried out, "No!" threw down his bundle of kindling, drew *Harbinger* from its sheath, and sprang forward. Cairn clutched Lars' cloak and yanked his friend back. On *Rignil*, Yens shrieked out

to his countrymen, holding aloft his chained arms. Krüllig slammed into the two lead Straelings head on, knocking
them both to the ground and sending a hot red gout of blood
flying across the green slope. But other Straelings swarmed
in to take the place of the two who fell. The Sea Wolf spun
right, tripping up two warriors before cleaving left, killing
one man with a single blow to the neck.

Thay got a fire going among the kindling on *Rignil's* deck and
he fed more brush into it. "Let me go to him, Cairn!" Lars bellowed, struggling against the big lad's grip. As Thay tossed larger
pieces of wood onto the deck, he looked up to see Krüllig lodg-
ing his axe into another man's chest, though more Straelings
swarmed down the hill. Five men had fallen to Krüllig's axe, but
he was now encircled by enemies and more than a dozen raced
towards the boats. The Fjordlander twisted and confronted new
opponents but Thay knew that the man had sacrificed himself.
He prayed that the sacrifice would mean something.

And with that thought, something changed in Thay's mind.
As the fire in *Rignil* gained strength, he scrambled over to Lars
who continued to struggle against Cairn's grip. "Lars! Do your
duty," he ordered. Lars stopped struggling and stared at Thay.
"Take a brand. Help us set *Northern Fire* alight."

Lars stared into Thay's eyes. "He's my oar mate," he cried.

"And he's saving your life," Thay snapped back, "and protecting his folk. Help him. Help us." Lora came running back
from *Thunderer*, black smoke already filling the sky behind her.

Lars clenched his teeth, heaved in a deep breath, nodded
and hissed, "Aye, I'll light a northern fire."

An odd look crossed Lora's face and she said, "It'll set the
world ablaze."

Lars re-sheathed *Harbinger*, he and Cairn each pulled a brand
from the fire and darted off to *Northern Fire*. Despite the growing blazes, Thay could barely see Lora's face against the black
clouds looming above the ships. "This storm feels like it's
directed at us," she cried as she threw more wood into the fire.

"You can't leave me to burn!" Yens shrieked down at them.

Thay felt like he was in one of his crimson dreams; a warmth flooded into his limbs from his heart and he yelled in response to Lora, "It's not directed at us, it's protecting us." Lars looked at Thay as though his friend had sprouted another head. "Just get the damn boats burning!" Thay called out. Lars nodded and continued hefting kindling onto *Thunderer's* deck.

"Don't let me get burnt alive!" Yens screamed again: his face had started to glow from the heat of the fire at the ship's prow.

Lora looked about and gasped, "Look at the river, and the storm. I've never seen the like of it." Thay gazed at the choppy waters, at the whipping grass and flooding black clouds, but Lars and Cairn kept glancing at the battle on the slope. Lars suddenly gave a cry and Thay knew that Krüllig had fallen. He stood back from his now blazing fire. He resisted looking up the hill and instead surveyed the progress that his friends had made. He saw small flames licking up from between *Thunderer's* gunnels and Cairn desperately fanning flames that appeared to dance around *Northern Fire's* ribs.

Thay hopped into *Rignil* and scampered to the stern, Yens lunging at his leg as he passed. "Don't let me burn!" Yens cried. Thay ignored the Straeling and carried on to the tiller, where he pried loose a small, locked chest anchored into the frame of the base of the rudder. Kindron kept Lora's *bondgyld* in the chest, silver that Uilig and Loska paid for keeping Lora safe, and Thay meant for it to achieve its purpose. And if there might be a bit more? - well, Kindron likely didn't want the treasure to go to waste.

"Unchain me!" Yens called. "I'll do nothing to harm you! Don't let me burn." Underneath the deck, the flames must have found a cask of whale oil for the planks exploded into flames. Yens shrieked again.

An arrow punched into the hull beside Thay and he threw himself behind the gunnel in surprise. He fumbled through the chest, found what he sought and closed it again. He heard the loud, harsh screaming of battle cries. Mustering his courage, he lunged to his feet and again ran down *Rignil's* length to Yens. None of the enemies managed a shot at him. He dropped a key onto Yens' lap and darted back to the stern.

"My bow! Thay, grab my bow!" Lora shouted to him above the racket of the storm. He snatched up the bow and Lora's quiver of arrows and tossed them down to her. Then he did the same with Cairn's maul, *Orgor's Awl*. Finally he hopped into the choppy river, pulled his dagger from its sheath and slashed at the rope that lashed the ship's dinghy to the hull. He pulled the boat free one handed - he still clutched Kindron's small chest - and heaved it onto the river where it bounced over the waves like a cork. Neither Lora nor Lars needed Thay to tell them what he intended, and they splashed headlong into the water, bent over the gunnels of the lifeboat and spun into it. Thay hoisted them the chest, threw them a couple of bags of gear, pulled another onto his back before pulling Cairn into the river. He thrust Cairn into the boat, causing it to list dangerously away from the burning *Rignil*, but Thay braced himself and then thrust off from shore. Yens suddenly appeared above them on *Rignil's* deck beside the tiller, an oar in his hands brandished like a lance. The Straeling heaved back his arm to throw the oar at them, but at that very instant the world flashed into a blaze of emerald and thunder exploded in their ears.

"Sk'van's Eye!" Thay swore as he heaved the dinghy into deep water. It caught the river's current and passed under the wooden bridge. Looking back over his shoulder, he saw that lightning must have hit *Northern Fire*, for it had exploded. What remained of its burning hulk obscured the far bank and the Straelings amassed there. He caught a glimpse of Yens pitching himself into the river just ahead of the spreading flames on *Rignil*.

The young Fjordlanders bobbed through the chop and sped down river, away from their attackers with only the flaring light of the three burning vessels illuminating their way. A few arrows struck the water behind and beside them, but the sudden storm and the pull of the current put the shot beyond the skill of any among those on shore. When Thay finally pulled himself into the small boat, he knew they were alone.

Epilogue

"You! Prepare to meet Galivith!" barked a man-at-arms over the howling of the wind among the trees, the lapping of the waves against the riverbank, and the echoes of thunder among the hills. On this strangest of days, with the eerie storm wreaking havoc across the valley of the Tamas River, the inner voice that sometimes spoke to Yens snapped him from his stupor. *Defend yourself!* As if to emphasize the voice, thunder boomed and a sickly green bolt of lightning rent the sky.

Yens' arms craft took over; he bent away from a spear thrust and retreated to higher ground. "Can you not see I'm Straelish?" he yelled. That gave the attacker pause. As the reverberations of that last blast of thunder died and as wind and wave filled the void, Yens added, "You've rescued a *herg*! Kill me and you're dead. Aid me and you're rich men."

More spearmen closed around him, warily, and then a swordsman stepped forward, bloody blade held low. "A *herg*?" The man's eyes sparkled, either reflecting the strange storm raging above them or simple greed.

"Aye," Yens replied. "*Herg* Yens Hezteins, from Freimund in Deltenlanden. Who are you and to whom are you sworn?" His voice shed all of the cowed subservience that self-preservation had taught him over the past years.

"I am Kimich Hummelz, sworn to *Oberherg* Skindler of Midelstrael," the swordsman said. "I am the captain of his *weroth*." It had been a long time since Yens had heard that word. *Weroth*: personal war band, elite body guard, household troops.

"Take me to your liege." Yens' order brooked no protest. When he saw the captain turn to organize his men-at-arms, he added, "And get me a coat."

The captain narrowed his eyes and came closer. "Southerners fetch their own coats when they're in Midelstrael. Or will fetching you one will make me a rich man?"

"Show a *herg* of the realm his due respect."

"I don't see no *herg*. I see a sodden piece of flotsam from a Thornish wreck, and I'll keep seeing sodden flotsam until I know you are who you say you are. You're lucky I see what I think is Straelish flotsam, not Thornish."

Yens cursed under his breath. He had been away from Straeland's shores so long that he hadn't immediately recalled the age-old hostility between his native land and neighbouring Midelstrael. Only recently in comparison to the long march of time had the seven ancient Straelish kingdoms been unified by the current Queen's grandfather, Hendl the Strong. Suspicion of the other remained strong while memories of past wrongs endured. Clearly Captain Hummelz was ill-inclined to celebrate Yens' freedom, and, as captain of a *weroth* to an *oberherg*, was likely nobility himself.

Hummelz stomped off to see if his men could salvage anything from the wreckage of the three longships. Yens could see easily enough that the effort was futile. Two of the longships had burned down to the waterline. The other one, *Northern Fire*, was only a submerged stern and stumps of charred wooden ribs splayed out like a cod for drying. The strangeness of that ship's demise – lightning having flashed down from the unnatural, green-tinted storm clouds to blast the ship apart – made him look up at the odd weather. The bank of clouds was thinning and the wind was dying down.

Captain Hummelz assembled the troops and they marched up the hill. They had a grim task of recuperating five bodies of fallen comrades up near the ridge line. Hummelz ordered the body of the dead Thorn, Krüllig, be stripped and left to the crows. Yens stepped forward and kicked the dead man's torso twice before Hummelz pulled him back.

As they marched across the uplands towards a forest in the near distance, the realization grew in Yens that he was no longer a slave. He felt his heart constricting his throat and a sob pounding against his ribs. It was over. It was truly over. For three years he had been a shackled slave, pulling an oar through sun, sleet, and swell, never given a coat or a blanket, never given a bite more than he needed to survive, never given a measure of mercy. He had endured the gloating of captors after their sadistic raids on his homeland, hearing about the slaughter of his folks and about the riches stolen from Straelish towns and temples.

Those thoughts, as ever they did, took him back to his own capture. Beaten and with open wounds welling blood into the longboat into which he had been tossed, he had looked back to the strand below the berg of Freimund and had seen his wife rise from where she had been violated on the stony beach. She had snatched a dagger from beneath the belt of that beast who had so brutally dealt with her, Hossig, and she had stabbed it into his arm. Hossig would've killed her had Albig, *Northern Fire's* captain, not laughed and ordered him back to the longboat. The last image he had of his home was of his wife's expression on that stony strand: forlorn, broken, watching her husband's abductors putting to sea.

But now it was over. He was free. He could return home, take Roderika in his arms, and beg her forgiveness. He dragged a sleeve across his eyes feeling dampness seep into the wool.

As they neared the woods, Hummelz ordered his men to help pile corpses and dig graves. Then he took Yens over to a thin, finely dressed nobleman of around forty years-of-age with a shock of sweat-dampened black hair plastered against his head. The captain gave a bow and gave his report. The nobleman cursed when he heard the ships couldn't be salvaged. Hummelz concluded, "Four Thorns escaped down-river in a rowboat. And we came across this fellow among the wreckage. Claims he's a Strael. Speaks like it and he doesn't look like a Thorn person. Says he's a *herg*."

The nobleman, *Oberherg* Skindler flicked a forefinger twice, summoning Yens into his presence. Yens stepped forward, bowed, and waited to be addressed. Skindler looked Yens over, no doubt seeing a bedraggled peasant with as many welts and bruises as all his men-at-arms combined. "If you are a Strael and sailed with these Thorns, then you can help us here. Tell me, are there other ships ... lurking ... in the hills? How many were in the raiding party?"

Yens said, "No more ships. There were one-hundred and forty-six Thorns. Your man mentioned the four who got away on a rowboat: those ones are young and inexperienced, but two of them can speak our tongue."

Skindler nodded. "I'll send out teams of riders. We'll track them down. Help Hummelz here with the count. We'll talk again when our task is done."

Yens was about to protest that he was a *herg* and above dealing with corpses, but he thought the better of it, especially if Hummelz, too, was of noble birth. As he worked, Yens was surprised to realize there were only a few Straels amongst the fallen and he said as much to the captain. "How did you know to bring so many men?"

Hummelz spat on the pile of Thornish bodies. "We had word of them two days past, having been seen by one of *Herg* Merner's shepherds the afternoon before. My master brought forth not only his own *weroth* but those of his vassals' between Battalberg and here. We've over five-hundred men ... or we did. We lost five in the pursuit of that bastard you kicked and I see the lads are digging over a dozen graves. More dead than that scum deserved to claim."

"But they had three shiploads of warriors!" Yens said. "And killing's in the nature of each and every one of them. A dozen dead is ... well, it's a miracle of Galivith! How could such a thing come to pass?"

The captain shrugged. "They came quickly and they didn't even have scouts out ahead of the main party. We jumped them in the woods. It was butchery more than anything. Their leader, this one ..." he rolled over the body of Kindron Sopallig with his foot, "...stepped out from their circle and called out a challenge, I think, but we stuck him with arrows. Their priest chanted some prayers, but Galivith is stronger than any Thornish god, so it did no good, though maybe it saved his life. He's lying over there."

The final count came up short a man. They did the count again while Skindler sent search parties into the woods. Again the count came up one short. The soldiers searched and searched but found no one hiding curled underneath roots or nestled among branches. Yens studied all the bodies lying on the grass and then looked at the dozen fallen Straels. His eyes followed the movements of two of Skindler's men lowering a brother-in-arms into a grave. The dead man's dun shirt looked odd, darker in the chest and shoulder, paler along the sleeves and tail. No tunic.

Suddenly he declared, "Their bard."

Yen's exclamation caught the attention of those working nearby the graves, including Skindler. The *oberherg* drew up and asked, "Bard?"

"Yes. A man called Erig. He's a cunning sort. *Oberherg*, assemble your troops!"

A gleam came into the *oberherg's* eyes and he turned to Hummelz. "Do as he suggests, captain. Assemble the men."

Soon rank upon rank of men-at-arms stood in the shade of the trees, out of the sun that had chased away all the storm clouds. Yens walked along the lines of men, studying faces, ordering one man wearing a helm to remove it. When he came to the last line, that closest to the eaves of the forest, someone in the middle of the formation broke and darted into the trees. Yens caught sight of yellow hair spilling from beneath a helm. "Get him!" he hollered, though the order was unnecessary; a dozen warriors bounded off after the fugitive.

Shortly thereafter the triumphant pursuers returned with their prize. Hummelz pulled off the helm and tossed it to a subordinate. Erig was wiry rather than bulky and he could not resist as he was driven onto his knees before the *oberherg*. The Thorn's cleverness had nearly saved him but nothing would save him now. Yens grinned in delight, the first joy he had felt in three years.

"You are an odd bard," Skindler said, glancing at the Fjordlander. "In this land, mummers don't risk their precious fingers in anything so ... dangerous ... as a raid."

Erig said nothing and drew himself as erect as the hands driving him onto his knees allowed. However brave the show, Yens saw fear behind those ice blue eyes. He translated Skindlers' comments into the Fjordlander tongue and saw the fear grow in Erig.

"I like music," Skindler continued. "I have a great collection of instruments mounted on the wall of my feasting hall. Now I have something to add to my collection. I shall take you with me so you can see those instruments and know you'll never be able to play them again."

After Yens had again relayed the words to Erig, the Fjordlander changed. Facing death well was one thing; fearing torture was another. The Thorn gibbered. Again Yens translated, "He say he'll play for you. He begs you not to break his fingers or lop off his hands. But I say do it! He deserves no better."

"What good would a slave be to me without his hands?" Skindler observed, "Although breaking the fingers might not be a bad idea." He pursed his lips and came to a decision. "Get him digging graves." Hummelz dragged Erig away.

Oberherg Skindler turned to Yens then. "You and I can speak now. Who are you?"

And so, Yens told his tale. A raid in the depths of winter, furious and without warning, the keep overwhelmed, slaughter, flame, and rape. The keep's wounded *herg* kept alive for sport and humiliation: a noble wife left weeping on the beach. Then years of slavery and labour. However, Skindler had little interest in hearing the details of Yens' time as a captive, interrupting, "You say your liege is *Oberherg* Yallberg. If that is so, tell me something about him. Is he tall, fat, balding, cross-eyed? Is he quick of wit? Does he limp when he walks?"

"He's vain and corrupt," Yens said, immediately and without thought.

Skindler's face lit up and he roared in laughter. "You really do know him!" Then he grew serious and said, "Walk with me." Skindler took Yens away from his troops. The *oberherg* had been cold, efficient, decisive. Now he carried himself differently; languid, less-aloof, a thoughtful look on his face. He said, "I heard about that raid. My wife's a southerner and she brought me news of it and of what followed. I'm sorry to say you're a *herg* no longer ... and that you're a widower."

"Wha ... what?"

"*Oberherg* Yallberg granted your demesne to your brother. Your lady wife threw herself from the cliff above your town shortly afterwards. I'm sorry."

Yens' legs gave way. He fell to his knees and he hung his head in his hands. His body heaved with the wave of sobs that wracked him. After some time, when the spasms subsided and his wailing died down, he felt a chest against his forehead and an arm about his shoulders. He swallowed and looked up through watery eyes. The *oberherg* was kneeling on the grass with Yens. Skindler's tunic showed dampness from Yens' weeping.

"Come, brother," Skindler said, standing and taking hold of Yen's arm. "On your feet. Come with me and I'll see you right. Galivith has seen fit to spare your life and bring you back to Straelish lands. He might have designs for you that we cannot foresee. He might yet offer you a chance for you to take your revenge against those who wronged you."

The Fjordlander Gods

Fjordland has two chief Gods, one female, one male:

Rulla, Dealer of Fates, Mistress of Owls: When Orgor first crafted the world of men (see the lesser Gods), the Gods beheld His creation and desired dominion over it. To avoid strife among the many Gods, who will pit Their will against each other, Rulla thought to order this new world. She made runes representing the Domains and obliged each of Them to select one. Because She is one of the two greater Gods, all the lesser Gods bent to Her will in this except one (see Tanat, hereafter). Rulla continues to manifest Herself in Orgor's world; upon the birth of a mortal, She selects a slate with a specific rune upon it that will guide that Fjordlander's fate. Significant events or collisions with other Gods may in fact be a manifestation of Rulla taking an interest in guiding human events, or She may actually decide to select another rune for the mortal. Events will tell which is true. The selection of a rune is seen by Fjordlanders as a path set out for the individual, but it is up to the individual to walk that path.

Hondrig the Judge. At death, He sits in judgement over whether a Fjordlander lived up to the potential of the rune Rulla selected upon birth. He weighs on His scale the rune against the accomplishments of the mortal in question. Then He allots an appropriate place in the Afterworld depending on whether the Fjordlander made the most of his or her fate, or, whether he or she made little effort to do so. Hondrig may also decide to send the soul of the Fjordlander to Skalagg, the Netherworld. Like Rulla, Hondrig also manifests Himself in Orgor's world; He will guide events to His will within any Domain if He so chooses. Again, events will show Hondrig's hand.

Lesser Gods of varying potency also populate Fjordlander theology, including:

Asgear, God of the Waves, who commands the seas.

Florri, God of Good Fortune, who controls the whims of luck.

Guliveg, Tender of the Spark of Life. It is said She wanted the Domain of the Sea but had to choose Her rune after Asgear chose His. It is also said that to spite Asgear, She may intervene to save the ship-wrecked or sailors otherwise in peril, and thus She is revered by those who ply the waves. She decides whether or not to lend succour to those whose life hangs in the balance, be it mothers and infants at childbirth, the diseased, or even the foolhardy taking some rash risk. However, She rarely manifests Herself to those locked in battle, for war is the Domain of Karn.

Heligat, Ruler of Skalagg, the Domain of the Dead, the Netherworld. Those mortals judged by Hondrig as unworthy are sent to toil for Heligat in Skalagg until the breaking of the world. It is said the invocation of a curse attracts Her attention. She is also said to send demons into the world on Her missions.

Karn, the Goddess of War. Revels in the conduct of war and is known to guide the outcome of battles based on Her whims, often manifesting Herself via Her berserkers.

Norrgi, the Master of the Winds. An active God, He controls the weather borne upon the winds. Whereas many Fjordlander sailors respect and fear Asgear, they revere Norrgi as much as they do Guliveg, though they fear Him when he is wrathful.

Orgor, the Crafter, the God who took it upon Himself to build the world. He is worshipped by all crafters and builders.

Tanat the Rogue. God of Chaos and Mischief. He oft ruins the plans of the other Gods simply for His amusement. It is said His choosing of His Domain came after many other rune slates had been chosen by the other Gods. He scorned the choosing and oft writes his own runes, depending on His mood.

Zareth, Mistress of Desire: Goddess of love, lust, and ambition.

Other spirits inhabit the Godspace and manifest themselves in Orgor's world. One that appears in this work is:

Sk'van, the Twisted, the Master of the Dark, the greatest of all demons. He captures the souls of the living, before Hondrig's weighing, and tortures them before giving them over to Heligat.

Note: Fjordlanders will sometimes name their children after one of the Gods, though never the two chief Gods, nor Heligat.

Glossary

Bjerndyr: mythical werebear that lives in the high slopes of the Boldring Mountains. Folk tales say it steals sheep and misbehaving children. On Even Day and Darknight, the bjerndyr sheds its fur and takes human form so it can pass among Fjordlanders to plan its hunts for the coming season. The only way to kill it is to thrust an iron dagger or sword into its skull between its eyes.

Bondgyld: a sum of silver given by one person to another for the safe-keeping of a third. Often paid to families to foster a neighbour.

Brightnight: the celebration of the summer solstice and often used as a synonym for the solstice.

Darknight: the celebration of the winter solstice and often used as a synonym for the solstice.

Demesne: a landed estate in Straeland owned by a particular herg.

Even Day: the spring or autumn equinox.

Fylgja: a familiar, usually an animal embodying the spirit of a master.

Godspace: sky.

Hearthfire: the autumn celebration of the harvest celebrated on the first new moon after the autumn Even Day.

Herg: a feudal title used in Straeland to denote a man who is the owner of a demesne.

Kenning: a metaphoric compound expression in Fjordlander verse. Thus, swan of death might represent raven, king's acclaim might represent coronation, or Norrgi-song might represent wind.

Kunungr: a Fjordlander term used to denote a king, though Fjordland does not have such a ruler.

Lifgyld: a sum of silver, or life price, given by one person to another in payment for a life-saving deed. It is also the sum a Fjordlander must pay to the Sea Wolves to muster out of the Unsettled Clan.

www.ingramcontent.com/pod-product-compliance
Lightning Source LLC
Chambersburg PA
CBHW020646260626
47157CB00008B/2933